HUSH MONEY

PARKER

ROBERT B.

HUSH MONEY

G. P. PUTNAM'S SONS

NEW YORK

G. P. PUTNAM'S SONS
Publishers Since 1838
a member of
Penguin Putnam Inc.
375 Hudson St.
New York, NY 10014

ISBN 0-399-14458-7

Printed in the United States of America

For Joan:

all the day and night time.

HUSH MONEY

CHAPTER ONE

Outside my window a mixture of rain and snow was settling into slush on Berkeley Street. I was listening to a spring training game from Florida between the Sox and the Blue Jays. Joe Castiglione and Jerry Trupiano were calling the game and struggling bravely to read all the drop-ins the station had sold. They did as well as anyone could, but Red Barber and Mel Allen would have had trouble with the number of commercials these guys had to slip in. The leisurely pace of baseball had once been made for radio. It allowed the announcers to talk about baseball in perfect consonance with the rhythm of the game. We listened not only to hear what happened but because we liked the music of it. The sound of a late game from the coast, between two teams out of contention on a Sunday afternoon in August, driving home from the beach. The crowd noise was faint in the background, the voices of the play-by-play guys embroidering on a dull game. Now there was little time for baseball talk. There was barely time for play-by-play. And much of the music was gone. Still, it was the sound of spring, and it took some of the chill out of the slush storm.

Just after the fifth inning started, Hawk came into my office with a smallish man in a short haircut, wearing a dark three-piece suit and a red and white polka dot bow tie. His skin was blue black and seemed tight on him. I turned the radio down, but not off.

"Client," Hawk said.

"Ever hopeful," I said.

I recognized the small man. His name was Robinson Nevins. He was a professor at the university, the author of at least a dozen books, a frequent guest on television shows, and a nationally known figure in what the press calls The Black Community. *Time* magazine had once referred to him as "the Lion of Academe."

"I'm Robinson Nevins," he said and put his hand out. I leaned forward and shook it without getting up. "Hawk may be premature in calling me a client. We need to talk a bit first, among other things we ought to find out if we can get along."

"Whose tab?" I said to Hawk.

"Guarantee half everything I get," Hawk said.

"That much," I said.

"I can't afford very much," Nevins said.

"Maybe we won't get along," I said.

"I am dependent largely on a university salary and, as I'm sure you know, that is not a handsome sum."

"Depends what sums you're used to," I said. "How about the books?"

"The books are well received, and have influence I hope beyond their sales. Their sales are modest. I make some money on the lecture circuit, but far too often I speak because I feel the cause is just rather than the price is right."

"Don't you hate when that happens," I said.

Nevins smiled, but not as if he thought I was funny.

"What would you like to pay me a modest amount to do?" I said.

"I have been denied tenure," Nevins said.

I stared at him.

"Tenure?" I said.

"Yes. Unjustly."

"And you want me to look into that?" I said.

"Yes."

"Tenure," I said.

"Yes."

I was silent. Nevins didn't say anything else. I looked at Hawk.

"You want me to do this?" I said to Hawk.

"Yes."

I was silent again.

"I understand your reaction," Nevins said. "I sound churlish to you. And you think that there are causes of greater urgency than whether I get tenure at the university."

I pointed a finger at Nevins. "Bingo," I said.

"I know, were I you that would be my reaction. But it is not simply that I am denied tenure and therefore will have to leave. I can find another job. What is at issue here is that I shouldn't have been denied tenure. I am more qualified than most members of the tenure committee. More qualified than many who have received tenure."

"You think it's racial?" I said.

"It would be an easy supposition and one most of us have made correctly in our lives," Nevins said. "But I am, in fact, not sure that it is."

"What else?" I said.

"I don't know. I am something of an anomaly for a black man at the university. I am relatively conservative."

"What do you teach?"

"American literature."

"Black perspective?"

"Well, my perspective. I include black writers, but I also include a number of dead white men."

"Daring," I said.

"Do you know that we are turning out English Ph.Ds who have never read Milton?"

"I didn't know that," I said. "You think you were shot down for being insufficiently correct?"

"Possibly," Nevins said. "I don't know. What I know is there was a smear campaign orchestrated by someone, which I believe cost me tenure."

"You want me to find out who did the smearing?"

"Yes."

I looked at Hawk again. He nodded.

"Wouldn't an attorney be more likely to get you your tenure?"

"I am not fighting this because I didn't get tenure. I'm fighting this because it's wrong."

"If you got the tenure decision reversed, would you accept it?"

Nevins smiled at the question.

"You press a person, don't you," he said.

"I like to know things," I said.

"Like how sincere I am about fighting this because it's wrong."

"That would be good to know," I said.

"If I were offered tenure I would have to assess my options. But even if I accepted it, the process was still wrong."

"What was the thrust of the smear campaign?"

Hawk appeared to be listening to the faintly audible ball game. And he was. If asked, he could give you the score and recap the last inning. He would also be able to tell you everything I said or Nevins said and how we looked when we said it.

"A young man, a graduate student, committed suicide this past semester. It was alleged to be the result of a sexual relationship with me."

"What was his name?" I said.

"Prentice Lamont."

"Any truth to it?"

"None."

I nodded.

"I imagine you'd like that laid to rest as well."

"Yes."

"Okay," I said.

"Okay meaning you'll do it?"

"Yep."

Nevins seemed mildly puzzled.

"Like that?"

"Yep."

"Aren't you going to ask if I'm gay?"

"Nope."

"Why not?"

"Don't care."

"But," Nevins frowned, "it might be germane."

"If it is, I'll ask," I said.

Nevins opened his mouth and closed it and sat back in his chair. Then he took a green-covered checkbook out of his inside coat pocket.

"What will you need for a retainer?"

"No need for a retainer," I said.

"Oh, but I insist. I don't want favors."

Hawk was looking out the window at the slush accumulating around the stylishly booted ankles of the young women leaving the insurance companies on their way to lunch.

Without turning around he said, "He doing me the favor, Robinson."

Nevins was not slow. He looked once at Hawk, and back at me, and nodded to himself. He put the green checkbook back inside his coat and stood.

"Do you need anything else right now?" he said.

"No. I'll poke around at it, see what develops."

"And I'll hear from you?"

"Yes," I said.

"Will you be involved, Hawk?"

Hawk turned from the window and grinned at Nevins.

"Sure," he said. "I'll help him with the hard stuff."

Nevins put out his hand. "I appreciate your taking this," he said, "for whomever you're doing the favor."

I shook it.

"You need a ride anyplace?" he said to Hawk.

Hawk shook his head. Nevins nodded as if to confirm something in his head, and turned and left. Hawk continued to look out the window. The ball game had moved quietly into the eighth inning. Outside my window it was mostly rain now. Hawk turned away from the window and looked at me without expression.

"Tenure?" I said.

Hawk smiled.

"'Fraid so," he said.

CHAPTER TWO

Susan periodically undertook to make my office more homelike, and one of her most successful attempts was the relatively recent introduction of a coffeemaker, coffee canisters, and some color-coordinated mugs. Milk for the coffee then required a small refrigerator, in which I could also keep beer in case of an emergency. The refrigerator, of course, matched the mugs and the canisters and the sugar bowl and milk pitcher. The coffee filters and flatware were in a little drawer in the cabinet that I had built under her direction to hold the refrigerator. Hawk always smiled when he looked at it. Which he was doing now as he made us some coffee.

"Surprised Susan don't have you color-coordinating your ammunition," Hawk said.

"Well, she does sort of like the .357," I said, "because she likes how the lead nose of the bullets contrasts with the stainless steel cylinder."

"Tasteful in small things," Hawk said, "tasteful in all things."

He poured a pot full of water into the coffeemaker and turned the machine on.

"Tell me about Robinson Nevins," I said.

"Father is Bobby Nevins," Hawk said.

"The trainer?"

"Un huh."

Hawk and I both watched the small trickle of coffee that Mr. Coffee was generating very slowly into the pot.

"A watched pot never brews," I said.

"Yeah it will," Hawk said.

"You know Bobby Nevins?" I said.

"Yeah."

"He ever train you?"

"Some," he said.

"That how you know the kid?"

"Un huh."

The pot had filled slowly.

"Tole you it would brew," Hawk said.

"Jeez," I said. "I was sure I was right."

Hawk took it from the machine and poured us two cups of coffee.

"You are a domestic fool," I said when Hawk handed me a cup.

"Ancestors were house slaves," Hawk said. "It's in the genes."

"So how well you know Robinson Nevins?" I said.

"Bobby come closer to bringing me up," Hawk said, "than anyone else."

"So you've known Robinson all your life."

"Yes."

"Well?"

"No, not so much. He was around some."

"But he came to you when he got in trouble," I said.

Hawk shook his head.

"Bobby did," Hawk said.

"He's still alive?"

"Yeah. Eighty-two now, still healthy, still hangs out at the gym looking for young fighters."

"So Robinson was born to him late."

"Yes, only kid. Got divorced when Robinson was pretty small. Wasn't a good divorce. Don't know where Robinson's mother is now."

"Kid close to his father?"

"Bobby loves that kid," Hawk said. "Kid grew up mostly with his mother. But Bobby paid the bills and saw the kid when he could and when the kid got to be a professor Bobby was walking around talking like the kid had just become heavyweight champ. You know, I don't know if Bobby ever even went to school. I'm not sure how much Bobby can read.''

"How about Robinson. He close to Bobby?"

"I think he's a little embarrassed by his father," Hawk said. "He's close to his mamma and his mamma never had much good to say about Bobby."

I nodded.

"What do you know about his problems?" I said.

"Just what he told you."

"What do you think?"

"'Bout the tenure or the suicide or what?"

"Any of the above," I said.

"Don't know shit about tenure," Hawk said. "Kid who died, Prentice Lamont, was a very gay guy. I pretty sure Robinson knew him. Don't know if Robinson is gay or not."

"How gay?" I said.

"Activist. Ran a little flier service that outed people."

"How nice," I said. "What's the rumor about him and Robinson?"

"That they had a big affair and Robinson broke it off and the kid killed himself."

"Love unrequited?"

"That's the rumor," Hawk said.

"Bobby Nevins know this rumor?"

"Yeah."

"What's he say?"

"He says fix it," Hawk said. "He wants the kid to get his tenure."

"Bobby got any money?"

Hawk shook his head. He was holding the coffee mug in both hands, his hips resting against the color-coordinated countertop, the steam from the coffee rising faintly in front of his face.

"So we're in this for the donut," I said.

Hawk nodded and smiled. When he smiled he looked like a large black Mona Lisa, if Mona had shaved her head . . . and had a nineteen-inch bicep . . . and a 29-inch waist . . . and very little conscience.

"How's that work, exactly," I said. "You take on somebody for no money, and I get to share in the profits?"

"You the detective," Hawk said.

"True."

"Whereas," Hawk said, "I just a simple thug."

"Also true."

"And you my friend."

"Embarrassing, but true."

"So." Hawk spread his hands, holding the coffee cup with his right, in a gesture of voilà. "I try to bring you as much business as I can."

"Like this thing."

"Exactly," Hawk said. "And I going to help you with it."

"Swell," I said.

"So what we going to do first?" Hawk said.

"Drink some more coffee," I said.

Hawk nodded. "Tha's a good start," he said. "Then what we going to do, bawse?"

"Get you diction lessons," I said. "I always know when you are really jerking my chain, because you start sounding like Mantan Moreland."

"Mantan Moreland?"

"I'm kind of proud of coming up with that one myself," I said. "Where did the Lamont kid do the deed?"

"Had a condo in the South End," Hawk said. "Did it there."

"Okay, that's Boston Homicide. Which means Quirk and Belson."

"So we talk with them first," Hawk said.

"I'll talk with them first," I said. "They'd arrest you."

"Bigots," Hawk said.

CHAPTER THREE

I was in Cambridge with Susan. We were cleaning up the back-yard behind the house on Linnaean Street where she lived and worked. Pearl the wonder dog was catching some rays on the top step of the back porch while we worked. Since part of what we were cleaning up was left by Pearl, it seemed only right that she be there.

I had dug a large hole in the recently thawed earth in one corner of the yard and into it I was putting shovelfuls of yard waste which Susan, wearing fingerless leather workout gloves, had raked into a number of small piles. One of the things that made Susan so interesting was the fact that she looked like a Jewish princess and worked like a Bulgarian peasant. As far as I knew she had never been tired. I dumped a shovelful of waste into the hole and shoveled a little dirt over it.

"Reminds me of my profession," I said.

"Cleaning up after?" Susan said.

"Yeah."

In addition to her workout gloves, Susan had on black tights, a hip-length yellow jacket, and a black Polo baseball cap. In the spirit of cleanup she had put on designer work boots, black leather with silver eyelets, which looked odd, but good, over the tights.

"It's a good reminder," Susan said, "of life's essential mess-iness."

"Or Pearl's."

"Same thing," Susan said.

Pearl raised her head slightly at the mention of her name, and then looked slightly annoyed that it was a false alarm. She sighed noisily as she settled her head back down onto her front paws. The sun was bright, and the earth had thawed, but in the shady corners against the fence and under a couple of evergreen shrubs, granular snow lingered like a dirty secret, and lurking inside the sixty-degree temperature was an edge of cold to remind us that it was too early for planting.

When we were done, and I had shoveled the dirt over the waste hole and tamped it down, Susan and I went and sat on the penultimate step, just below Pearl.

"Are you actually going to investigate that tenure case at the university?" Susan said.

"Yes."

She smiled.

"What," I said.

"The thought of you rampaging about in the university tenure committee," Susan said, "is very engaging."

"Rampaging?" I said. "I can be delicate as a neurosurgeon when it's called for."

"Most university tenure committees call for rampaging, I think."

"I admit to being more comfortable with that approach," I said.

Moved by an impulse understandable only by another dog, Pearl raised up and began to lap my face. I hunched up and endured it until she decided I'd had enough and switched to Susan.

"How'd you know about the case?" I said.

She was fending Pearl off, so it took her a while to answer. But finally, Pearl-free and makeup still mostly intact, Susan said, "Hawk discussed it with me, before he asked you."

"He did?" I said.

"He wanted my view on whether he was asking more of you than he should," Susan said.

"And you answered?"

"I answered that he had the right to ask you for everything and vice versa."

"What'd he say?"

Susan smiled.

"He agreed," she said.

I nodded.

"Is Hawk's friend gay?" Susan said.

"Don't know," I said.

"But wouldn't raging heterosexuality be a useful defense against the allegation that the graduate student killed himself as the result of an affair with Professor Nevins?"

"I guess it would," I said.

"Did you ask him?"

"No."

"I understand why you would not, but isn't it something that needs to be established?"

"Can it be established?" I said. "In my experience it's not always so clear-cut."

Susan leaned her elbows on the top step and pressed her head back against Pearl's rib cage. She thought about my question for a moment while I observed the way in which her posture made her chest press sort of tight against her jacket.

"Are you looking at my boobs?" Susan said.

"I'm a trained investigator," I said. "I notice everything."

"Do you make judgments on what you observe?"

"I try not to, but am sometimes forced to."

"And the boobs?"

"Top drawer," I said. "What about the question?"

"It's a good one," Susan said, "and much more complicated than is generally thought."

"Then I've come to the right place."

"Yes." Susan smiled at me. It was a smile that could easily have launched a thousand ships. "Complications R Us."

She rubbed the back of her head on Pearl for a moment.

"Sexuality is not as fixed as is commonly thought, and the discussion of it has become so political that if you quoted in public what I'm about to say I'd probably deny I said it."

"Before or after the cock crowed?" I said.

"I didn't know it crowed," Susan said.

"Never mind," I said. "Talk to me about sexuality."

Susan smiled but didn't go for the obvious remark.

Instead, she said, "I have treated people who experienced themselves as homosexual at the beginning of therapy and experienced themselves as heterosexual at the end." Susan was picking her words carefully, even with me. "I have treated people who experienced themselves as heterosexual at the start of therapy and experienced themselves as homosexual at the end."

"And if you said that in print?"

"A fire storm of outrage."

"Because you seem to be saying that sexuality can be altered by therapy?"

"I am recounting my experience," Susan said. "Obviously I have experienced a self-selecting sample: people whose presence in therapy is probably related to either uncertainty about, or dissatisfaction with, their sexuality. It is not always the presenting syndrome, and it is not always what people thought they wanted. Some people come to be 'cured' of their homosexuality, only to embrace it by the end of the therapy."

I nodded. As she concentrated on what she was saying, Susan had stopped rubbing Pearl's rib cage with her head, and Pearl leaned over and nudged Susan with her nose. Susan reached up and patted her.

"And in the therapeutic community that would be unacceptably incorrect?" I said.

"I don't know anywhere, but here, that what I've said wouldn't stir up a ruckus."

"You've never minded a ruckus."

"No," Susan said. "Actually, I sometimes like ruckuses, but this ruckus would get in the way of my work, and I like my work better even than a ruckus."

"How about me," I said. "Do you like me better than a ruckus?"

"You are a ruckus," Susan said.

CHAPTER FOUR

I talked with Frank Belson in his spiffy new cubicle in the spiffy new police headquarters on Tremont Street in Roxbury.

"Golly," I said when I sat down.

"Yeah," Belson said.

"This will knock crime on its ear, won't it?" I said.

"Right on its ear," Belson said.

He was built like a rake handle, but harder. And, though I knew for a fact that he shaved twice a day, he always had a blue sheen of beard.

"They issue you a nice new gun when you moved here?"

"I could call informational services," Belson said. "One of the ladies there be happy to tour you around the new facility."

"Maybe later," I said. "What do you know about a suicide named Prentice Lamont?"

"Kid from the university?"

"Yeah."

"Did a Brody out the window of his apartment. Ten stories."

"A Brody?"

"Yeah. I heard George Raft say that in an old movie last week," Belson said. "I liked it. I been saving it up."

"Why?"

"Why'd he do a Brody?" Belson grinned. "Left a note on his computer. It said, I believe, 'I can't go on. There's someone who will understand why.'"

"What kind of suicide note is that?" I said.

"What, is there some kind of form note?" Belson said. "Pick it up at the stationery store? Fill in the blanks?"

"Did he sign it?"

"On the computer?"

"Well, did he type his name at the end?"

"Yeah."

"Any thought that maybe he got Brodied?"

"Sure," Belson said. "You know you always think about that, but there's nothing to suggest it. And when there isn't, we like to close the case."

"Any more on the cause?"

"We were told that he was despondent over the end of a love affair."

"With whom?"

"That's confidential information," Belson said.

"Who told you?"

"Also confidential," Belson said.

He reached into the left-hand file drawer of his desk and ruffled some folders and took one out and put it on his desk.

"That's why we keep all that information right here in this folder marked confidential. See right there on the front: Con-fid-fucking-dential."

He put the blue file folder on his desk, and squared it neatly in the center of the green blotter.

"I'm going down the hall to the can," Belson said. "Be about ten minutes. I don't want you poking around in this confidential folder on the Lamont case while I'm gone. I particularly don't want you using that photocopier beside the water cooler."

"You can count on me, Sergeant."

Belson got up and walked out of the squad room down the hall. I leaned over the desk and turned the file toward me and opened it. The report was ten pages long. I picked up the file and walked down to the copy machine and made copies. Then I went back to Belson's cubicle.

When Belson came back the copies were folded the long way and stashed in my inside coat pocket, and the file folder was neatly centered on Belson's blotter. Belson picked the folder up without comment and put it back in his file drawer.

"Unofficially," I said, "you got any thoughts about this thing?"

"I'm never unofficial," Belson said. "When I'm getting laid, I'm getting laid officially."

"How nice for Lisa," I said.

Belson grinned.

"I don't see anything soft in the case," he said. "The kid was gay, apparently had a love affair with an older man that went sour, and he did the, ah, Brody."

"You interview the older man?"

"Yep."

"He admit the affair?"

"Nope. He is a faculty member at the university. I heard he was up for tenure."

"So he'd have some reason to deny it."

"I don't know how they feel on the tenure committee about professors fucking students," Belson said. "You?"

"I'm guessing it's considered improper," I said.

"Maybe," Belson said.

"You ask?" I said.

Belson dropped his voice.

"The deliberations of the tenure committee are confidential," he said.

"So they wouldn't tell you if sex with a student counted for or against tenure?"

"Some of the people I talked to, sex with anything would count," Belson said.

"But you got no information from the tenure folks."

"No."

"And if you yanked their ivy-covered tuchases down here for a talk?" I said.

"Tuchases?"

"You can always tell when a guy's scoring a Jewess," I said.

"I thought the plural was tuch-i," Belson said.

"Shows you're not scoring a Jewess," I said. "You didn't want to shake them up a little?"

"We had no reason to think that the case was anything but an open and shut suicide," Belson said.

He smiled. "Quirk wanted to run them down here just because they annoyed him," he said. "But they had the university legal counsel there, and like I say, we had no reason."

"But it would have been kind of fun," I said.

Belson smiled but he didn't comment. Instead he said, "So what's your interest. You think the suicide's bogus?"

"Got no opinion," I said. "I been hired to find out why Robinson Nevins didn't get tenure."

"Really?" Belson said.

"He says a malicious smear campaign prevented it, including the allegation that he was the faculty member for whom Lamont did the Brody."

"See?" Belson said. "I knew you'd like that word. Does he admit it?"

"He denies it."

Belson shrugged.

"Should be easy enough to prove he had a relationship," Belson said.

"Harder to prove that he didn't."

"Yep."

I stood up.

"Well, I think your new digs are fabulous."

"Yeah, me too," Belson said.

"But it's a long way from Berkeley Street. What are you going to do when you need help?"

"You're as close as my nearest phone," Belson said.

"Well, that must be consoling to you," I said.

"Consoling," Belson said.

CHAPTER FIVE

At two in the afternoon the temperature was in the eighties, the sun was bright, and there was only a very soft breeze. A perfect midsummer day except that it was March 29. I was reading the paper with my feet up and the window open.

Susan came into my office wearing white shorts and a dark blue sleeveless top. She had Pearl on a leash.

"It's summer," she said. "I want us to go outside and play."

"Don't you have patients?" I said.

"Not this afternoon. It's the afternoon I teach my seminar."

"And?"

"And I canceled my seminar because of the weather."

"I might have clients," I said.

Susan glanced around my office.

"Un huh."

"And I might be studying evidence," I said.

She came around the desk and looked over my shoulder.

"Tank McNamara," she said.

"There could be a clue there," I said. "You don't know."

Susan gave me a look that, had it not been diluted by affection, would have been withering. I folded the paper carefully and put it down on my desk.

"So," I said, "what would you like to do?"

"You don't know where there's a field of daffodils in bloom, do you?"

"Susan," I said, "it's March 29."

"Okay, then let's walk along the river."

"Flexible," I said.

"You bet."

"I like flexible," I said.

"I know."

We were crossing the footbridge near the Shell when Susan said to me, "Do you have time between the Robinson Nevins case and Tank McNamara to do a little something for a friend of mine?"

I said I did.

"KC Roth," Susan said. "Actually that's a nickname. Short for Katherine Carole. She is recently divorced, and being stalked."

"Ex-husband?" I said.

"That's what she thinks, but she's not actually seen him."

"So how does she know she's being stalked?" I said.

We were down on the Esplanade, and Pearl was leading out up the river.

"Phone calls, she answers, silence at the other end," Susan said. "A flat tire, there's a nail in it; eerie music on her answering machine; a guy she dated got a threatening letter."

"Anonymously," I said.

"Of course."

"He keep it?"

"I don't know. She said she hasn't seen him since."

"Course of true love," I said, "never did run smooth."

Pearl saw a cocker spaniel coming along the Esplanade from the other direction. She growled. The hair on her back rose.

"Not a friendly dog," I said to Susan.

"Friendly to you and me," Susan said.

"All you can ask," I said. "What you've described may legally be stalking, but it falls more into the realm of dirty tricks."

"I know."

"Husband abuse her when he was with her?"

"I asked that," Susan said. "She says he did not."

"Why'd they divorce?"

"She left him for another man," Susan said.

"And the other man?" I said.

"Didn't work out."

"How come she doesn't think it's the other man doing the stalking?"

"He dumped her," Susan said.

"As soon as she became available?"

"Yes."

"You know his name?"

"No. She won't tell me, says he's a married man."

"Who was happy to sleep with her on the side and said 'oh honey if only we were single' and she believed him and got single."

"I don't know what happened," Susan said, "but your scenario is not unheard of."

The spaniel passed by and kept going with its owner. Pearl looked longingly after it and then stopped growling and let her hair back down and forged ahead again, keeping the leash taut.

"What's her ex's name?" I said.

"Burt—Burton. Burton Roth."

"You know him?"

"He seemed a pleasant man."

"Any kids?"

"One, she's with her father."

"Hmph," I said.

"Hmph?"

"Hmph."

"What's hmph mean?"

"Means now I've got two cases and no fee," I said.

"Well, in this case there might not exactly be *no* fee," Susan said.

"I'll get right on it," I said.

CHAPTER SIX

Hawk and I sat on a bench by the swan boat lagoon in the Public Garden on the first good day of spring. The temperature was 77. The sun was out. And the swan boats were cranking. We were looking at the notes I made from Belson's confidential files.

"So," Hawk said when we were through. "Nobody actually claims to have seen Robinson and the Lamont kid together in any romantic fashion except these two professors."

I looked at my photocopy of Belson's report.

"Lillian Temple," I said, "and Amir Abdullah."

"Amir," Hawk said.

He was looking at a squirrel who kept skittering closer to us, and rearing up and not getting anything to eat and looking as outraged as squirrels get to look.

"You know Amir?" I said.

"Yeah, I do," Hawk said.

"Tell me about him," I said. A man in an oversized double-breasted suit walked by eating peanuts from a bag.

"Gimme one of your peanuts, please," Hawk said.

The man in the big suit looked flustered and said, "Sure," and held the bag out to Hawk. Hawk took a peanut out and said, "Thank you." Big Suit smiled uncomfortably and walked on. Hawk gave the peanut to the squirrel and then said again, "Amir."

I waited.

"Amir embarrassed as hell he didn't grow up poor. And he

embarrassed as hell he lived where there was white folks and he been working for the Yankee dollar all his life.''

"Most of us do," I said.

"But Amir, he never had no ghetto to drag himself out of, and been treated decent by all the white folks he met along the way, and he got a scholarship and then he got another one and he got a nice middle-class income and now he got a Ph.D. and he can't stand it."

"Poor devil," I said.

"So to make up," Hawk said, "Amir so down even I don't understand him when he talk."

"So he'll be really pleased to help me with this investigation," I said.

"Can't hide the fact that you a blue-eyed devil, but I maybe talk to him with you," Hawk said. "Give you some, ah, authenticity."

The aggressive squirrel returned and looked at Hawk, sitting up on its hind legs, balancing on its disproportionate tail.

"Give a squirrel a peanut and you feed him for a moment," I said. "But teach him to grow peanuts . . .''

"You and Amir going to get along so good," Hawk said. "Can't wait to watch."

"How about Ms. Temple," I said, "I don't suppose you know her."

"How I going to know her?" Hawk said.

"Well, for a while you were running a sub-specialization in female professors," I said. "She coulda been one of them."

"Good-looking female professors," Hawk said.

"How do you know Prof. Temple isn't good-looking?"

"Don't," Hawk said. "But the odds are with me."

"Just because she's an academic?" I said.

"Where she live?" Hawk said.

I checked my notes. "Cambridge," I said.

Hawk smiled.

"Well, it doesn't actually prove she's not a looker," I said.

Hawk continued to smile.

"This is bigotry," I said. "You're generalizing based on profession and residence."

"Yowzah," Hawk said.

"She might be a beauty," I said.

"What you figure the chances of that are?" Hawk said.

I shrugged.

"Slim and none," I said.

Hawk smiled more widely.

CHAPTER SEVEN

I went to visit KC Roth. She was living in one unit of a brick complex of what used to be called garden apartments, on Route 28 in Reading. Across the street was a liquor store and a fish place called The Friendly Flounder. Up the street was what may have been the last drive-in movie theater in Massachusetts. Next to the garden apartments was an Exxon gas station and convenience store.

KC's apartment was neat enough, but it had been built for the builder's profit. The doors were hollow core. The finish work was minimal, mostly quarter round molding. The floors were plywood, covered wall to wall with inexpensive tan carpeting which didn't wear well, but showed the dirt easily. The furniture was fresh from the warehouse at Chuck's Rent-All, Everything for the Home.

"Well," KC said when I introduced myself, "so that's what you look like."

"This is it," I said.

"Susan spoke of you a lot, but I never knew what you looked like."

"But from the way she talked, you were picturing Adonis," I said.

"I guess," she said. "Come on in."

KC was wearing a man-tailored white shirt and blue jeans. She was amazingly good-looking. Thick black hair worn a little too long, large green eyes, wide mouth, flawless skin.

"You are so nice to come by," she said when we were sitting

in her ugly living room. "How about a nice cup of coffee, or a drink? Do private eyes drink before lunch? I have some vodka."

"I don't need anything," I said. "Tell me about your problem."

"Oh boy, all business," she said.

She was sitting on the couch with her feet tucked up under her. I sat across in an uncomfortable barrel-shaped gray plush armchair.

"Well," I said, "not *all* business."

She smiled brilliantly. There was something about her that seemed to require flirtation. And when the requirement was filled, it pleased her.

"I'll keep it in mind," she said.

"So how about the harassment?" I said.

"The son of a bitch won't give up," she said. "Can you make him stop?"

"The son of a bitch being whom?"

"Burt, the bastard—I hope you don't mind swearing, I can't help it, I have a terrible mouth."

"I'll be all right," I said. "Burt is your husband?"

"*Ex*-husband," she said.

"And you know he's doing this?"

"Who else." She leaned forward and her voice became a little girl's. "Could you beat him up for me?"

She had more affect than a Miss America contestant. Her voice went from contralto to soprano in an easy glissade. Her eyes widened and narrowed as she spoke. Everything she said, she dramatized. She went from seductress to child in an exhale. I was willing to bet she'd cry before I left. I was pretty sure she could cry at will.

"We'll see," I said. "Could anyone else be harassing you?"

She cast her eyes down.

"No," she said softly. "Who else but Burt would have any reason?"

"Tell me about your boyfriend," I said.

She kept her eyes downcast and was silent. It was a pose, but I didn't think it was an insincere one. In fact I didn't find her insincere at all. Rather she seemed to have been playing this role, whatever it was, for so long, that she probably didn't have any idea when she was sincere and when she wasn't.

"I can't talk about him," she said.

"Why not?" I said.

She raised her head and she was angry, or seemed to be.

"I'm not hiring you to cross-examine me."

"You're not hiring me at all, yet," I said. "This is foreplay. See if we like each other."

"You only work for people you like?"

"I only work for people I want to," I said.

She smiled suddenly. It was quite spectacular.

"You'll want to work for me," she said.

"So what about the boyfriend?"

The smile went away.

"Must you?"

"'Fraid so," I said.

"Is it confidential?"

"Absolutely," I said. "But it's not privileged."

"What do you mean?"

"If you hired me through your attorney," I said, "under certain circumstances what you told him, and he told me, could be privileged. As it stands now, I won't tell anyone, but it is not privileged. If it is information required by the police in the course of an investigation, or a prosecutor in the course of a trial, then if I'm asked I have to tell."

"Police?"

"I'm just trying to be clear," I said. "I don't expect to tell anyone."

"If you told anyone I'd die."

"I'll try to remember that."

We were quiet. She was thinking, and, as she did everything else, she dramatized thinking. Her eyes narrowed, she got a vertical wrinkle between her eyebrows. Her lips pursed slightly. I waited. Finally she leaned back and shifted on the couch so that she could hug her knees while she talked.

"When we were together," she said, "we could barely breathe. We couldn't eat. We didn't want to drink. All we wanted to do was be together and look at each other and make love."

I nodded. I knew the feeling, though love had never made me lose my appetite.

"If only we were both free," she said.

"You're free," I said.

She shook her head sadly and a little condescendingly.

"He can't leave his wife."

"Why?"

She shook her head again. Men were so dumb.

"He just can't. She's too dependent on him, and men can't do the hard things. He's such a baby."

"Might have been smart to wait until he left her, before you left your husband," I said.

"I'm not that way," she said. "When I commit, I commit entirely. I give everything."

"Would you have left your husband if you hadn't thought you'd be with him?" I said.

"And what? Live in this gruesome goddamned apartment by myself? Burt and I lived in a castle."

"Do you still see your boyfriend?" I said.

Again the downcast eyes. Her mouth pouting like a sad child, albeit a cute one, she traced a small circle on her kneecap with the forefinger of her right hand.

"No."

"Why not?"

She began to cry. I waited, letting the question hang. She placed both her hands over her face, being careful of her makeup, and cried some more. I was pretty sure I was supposed to go and sit on the couch and put my arm around her, in which case she would turn in and bury her head on my shoulder and weep as if her heart would break. I stayed where I was. Finally after waiting as long as was decorous she stopped crying and lowered her hands, and raised her head so she could look searchingly into my eyes.

"Men are such babies," she said.

"Maybe not all of them," I said.

"You're not, are you?"

"Except when I don't get my way," I said. "How come you and the BF are not still an item?"

"Somehow, I know this sounds . . . something . . . anyway, somehow when we were both married and sleeping with each other it was, like even. But then I was divorced and he was the only one that was cheating. He couldn't stand it."

It did in fact sound . . . something.

"Sure," I said. "What is his name?"

"Oh, I can't give you his name," she said.

"You can if you wish me to work for you."

"Aren't you already hired, I mean, I've told you all this stuff."

"KC, the surest way to prevent the stalker involves knowing who he is. Probably is your ex-husband; but it might be your ex-boyfriend, it might be somebody else. If I'm going to do what you are trying to hire me to do, I will do it better and quicker if you tell me what I ask."

She bit her lower lip gently and, with her hands laced over her knees, rocked slightly on the couch.

Finally she said, "Louis."

"That's a start," I said.

More lower-lip biting until finally she said, quite tragically, I thought, "Vincent."

"Louis Vincent," I said.

Her voice softened almost reverentially. "Yes."

"And where does he live?"

"Hingham."

"Does he have a place of business?"

"Why?"

"Doesn't seem discreet to approach him at home," I said.

"Oh God, you can't approach him. He'd never forgive me."

"He'll never know I got it from you," I said.

Again a long and fully acted out period of silent pondering.

"He's a stockbroker," she said. "Hall, Peary."

"Fifty-three State," I said.

She nodded. I had made her thoroughly miserable.

"Would you feel safer if I had someone outside your house until I, ah, crack the case?"

"I went down to the police department," she said. "The sergeant was so nice, really lovely to me."

"I'll bet he was."

"He says they'll keep an eye on my apartment."

"Have you notified the phone company?"

"No."

She seemed startled, either that she hadn't thought of it, or that I had.

"You should probably do that," I said.

"He never says anything when he calls."

"Most people don't," I said.

If she thought I was amusing she didn't let on.

CHAPTER EIGHT

Hawk and I went to call on Amir Abdullah in his offices at the African-American Center at the university. A couple of hard-looking young guys in black suits and white shirts let us in. They eyed me like I was a case of the clap.

"Teaching fellows?" I said to Hawk.

Hawk smiled and let his stare rest on the two men.

"Dr. Abdullah," I said. "He's expecting me."

They looked at me some more and at Hawk, who smiled at them engagingly.

Then one of them said, "Down this hall, third door on the left."

Hawk and the two young men kept eye contact until we were past them and headed down the hall. There was African art on the walls, and some splashy posters advocating action. Everyone I saw was black.

"I feel like Casper the friendly ghost," I said.

"You a pale one, all right," Hawk said, and we knocked on the half-open door of Abdullah's office.

A voice said, "Come!" And in we went.

The walls of the office were covered with some sort of pan-African proletarian art in which magnificent black men were throwing off yokes of oppression. The white men in the posters were all mean-looking fat guys. None of the white guys looked like me. None of the magnificent black men looked like Abdullah. Abdullah was very light-skinned. In the old days, before tans were unhealthy, Susan, in summer, was darker than Amir.

He was skinny, and quite tall. His hair was short and militant-looking. He wore round gold glasses and a saffron-colored robe and sandals. His nails were long and clean and looked manicured. He wore rings on all four fingers of each hand. A Rolex watch peeked diffidently out from under the sleeve of his robe. He was smoking a long curved meerschaum pipe, and the room was rich with the pungency of his tobacco. A six-foot shield made of ornamented hide stood in the corner, with two long-bladed spears crossed over it. The bookcases were full of books. Many names I didn't recognize, a few I did, Frantz Fanon, Ralph Ellison, Richard Wright.

Abdullah nodded at Hawk.

"Do I know you?" he said to me.

"My name's Spenser," I said. "This is Hawk."

Abdullah looked thoughtfully at Hawk, and nodded.

"S'happenin,' bro?"

Hawk didn't say anything. He moved to the left of the door and leaned on the wall. Abdullah looked back at me.

"Don't get many white men in here," Abdullah said.

"Too bad," I said.

"Why?"

"I hate segregation," I said.

"Don't need no smartass honky jivin' me 'bout segregation," Abdullah said. "Nigger's got to get on with life. He do that best if he keep Whitey at a distance."

I didn't see anything there to help me with Robinson Nevins' tenure problem so I let it slide.

"You're on the English department tenure committee?" I said.

"Why you axin?"

The strain of talking like a homeboy was palpable in Abdullah, you could tell he had to rephrase things in his head so he wouldn't sound like Clarence Thomas. Leaning against the wall, Hawk looked like he was fighting a yawn.

"You caught me," I said. "Actually I know you're on the tenure committee of the English department, I guess I was really wondering why you don't have an office there."

"Ain't my business solvin' yo' problems," Abdullah said.

"Of course not," I said. "You ever see Robinson Nevins in a sexual circumstance with the late Prentice Lamont?"

"You ain't no cop," Abdullah said.

"How can you be sure?"

"You'da hassled me when you came in."

"Private cop," I said.

"And him." Abdullah nodded at Hawk.

"Amir," Hawk said. "You refer to me as 'him' again and I will slap your skinny ass around this office like a handball."

Hawk's voice was calm and his diction was better than Tony Blair's. Abdullah flushed. He was so light that it was visible.

"Only way you talk to a brother like that, is if you a damned Tom," Abdullah said.

Without a word Hawk stepped toward Abdullah, who flinched back involuntarily behind his desk.

"Hawk," I said. "It won't get us what we're after."

Standing directly at Abdullah's desk, Hawk kept his eyes on Abdullah.

"No white man calls me nigger," Hawk said quietly, "no black man calls me Tom."

He leaned across the desk and grabbed a handful of Abdullah's saffron robes. Abdullah screeched for help and several of the hard young men in dark suits came dashing down the corridor. Hawk slapped Abdullah across the face forehand and backhand, hard enough to rock his head back. Abdullah was all skinny arms and legs scrambling to get away. Hawk slapped him again as the first of the hard young men rushed into the room. Hawk dropped Abdullah, turned, and flattened the hard young man with a left hook. Three more crowded through the door. I took in a deep breath and let it out, and hit one of them on the back of his neck behind his right ear, and the fight was on. There were four of them and two of us, but one of us was Hawk and one of us was me, and they had Abdullah on their side. Having Abdullah on your side was like subtracting one, so the fight was almost even. The young men were all aficionados of some sort of Asian fighting technique, at which they were technically skilled. But they'd used it mostly to frighten college kids and intimidate professors. By the time the university cops arrived, the fight was over, we had won, and the militant Professor Abdullah was trying to crawl out of his office door from behind his desk, before Hawk got hold of him again.

"He assaulted me," Abdullah shrieked to the first cop through the door. "He assaulted me."

The university cops were followed in pretty close order by a couple of Boston cops, one of whom I knew. The university cops wanted to arrest us, but I explained what I was doing there and swore that Abdullah had started it, and the Boston cop that I knew interceded and eventually Hawk and I walked, though we were to stay close in case Abdullah pressed charges.

When we left the university police station we headed for the Harbor Health Club. After Henry Cimoli had stopped fighting, and before he opened what at that time he'd called a gym, on the waterfront, he'd worked corners for a while as a cut man. I had a cut under my eye, and a puffy lip and the knuckles on my left hand were scraped and swollen. Hawk had a black eye and a cut on his bald scalp that bled a lot. We needed Henry's repair service.

"Well," I said, "a fine mess you got us into this time, Ollie."

"He hurt my feelings," Hawk said.

He was pressing a folded paper towel against the cut on his head.

"You don't have feelings," I said. "I've heard blacks call you Tom, and whites call you nigger, and for all you cared they could have been singing 'Louie, Louie.' "

"I know."

"And all of a sudden you have a NO-BLACK-MAN-CALLS-ME-TOM fit and we're fighting four martial arts freaks."

"I know. Done good too," he said. "Didn't we."

"We're supposed to," I said. "What was all that wounded pride crap."

Hawk grinned.

"Scrawny fucker annoyed me," Hawk said.

"Well, of course he did," I said.

"Hate phonies," Hawk said.

"Sure," I said. "It's the right thing to do. But if it comes up again, could you hate them on your time?"

Atlantic Avenue was generously dug up and intricately detoured as the Central Artery project lumbered ahead. I pulled in and parked in among some heavy equipment near the Harbor Health Club.

"Can't promise nothing," Hawk said.

CHAPTER NINE

So far I was nowhere.

We had annoyed the hell out of Amir Abdullah but hadn't learned a thing. I had talked with KC Roth and hadn't learned much about that case, except that KC was a piece of work. I had talked with Belson and gotten nothing to help me. My next appointment was at the university with Professor Lillian Temple of the English department tenure committee, that afternoon at two. Until then I had nothing else to do except watch the swelling subside in my lip, so I decided to go up to Reading and talk with the cops about KC Roth. No grass growing under my feet. Two cases at a time. I thought about having "Master Sleuth" added to my business cards.

I talked to a beefy red-faced Reading police sergeant named O'Connor in the squad room.

"Yeah, we have a car go by there usually about every hour. It's easy enough, we routinely patrol that stretch anyway."

"You vary the time?" I said.

"We're just sort of shit-kicker cops out here, a course," O'Connor said, "but we did figure out that if we showed up the same time every night people might start to work around us."

"Good thinking," I said. "You have any thoughts on the stalker?"

"Like who he is?"

"Un huh."

"Well, the ex-whatever is usually the one you look at, if there is somebody."

"You have any reason to think there might not be a stalker?" I said.

"Well, you've talked to the lady," O'Connor said. "What's your impression?"

"Good-looking," I said.

"Yeah."

"Seems as if she might be sexually forthcoming," I said.

"You bet," O'Connor said.

"You got any information on that?"

"Nope, just instinct."

"Nice combo," I said. "Good-looking and easy."

"The best," O'Connor said, "if there wasn't the next morning to think about."

"That could be grim," I said. "But what's your point?"

"Just that she seems like she ain't wrapped too snug," O'Connor said. "Nothing about her bothered you?"

"She seemed a little contrived."

"Contrived? I heard you was a tough guy. Tough guys don't say contrived."

"Probably don't say sexually forthcoming either," I said.

"A course they don't," O'Connor said.

"Part of my disguise," I said. "So you haven't seen any sign of a stalker."

"No."

"Telephone records?"

"She hadn't talked to the phone company when we talked with her. They weren't keeping track."

"I suggested she do that," I said.

"We did too."

"Damn. She acted like I was smarter than Vanna White when I suggested it."

"Sure."

"So why would she make it up?" I said.

"You've seen broads like her, probably more than I have. Husband dumps them, they're alone out in the suburbs, and they want men around. They want to be looked after. So they call the cops a lot. Maybe Mrs. Roth just took it a step farther and hired a guy to look after her."

"Me," I said, "after you broke her heart."

"Could be."

"On the other hand, you look like her, you probably don't have to hire anyone," I said.

"After they get dumped," O'Connor said, "they're pretty crazy. Ego's fucked. Maybe she don't know she's good-looking."

"She knows," I said.

O'Connor thought about it for a minute. "Yeah," he said. "She does."

"And there's at least two ex-whatevers," I said.

"Boyfriend?" O'Connor said.

"Yep. Way she told me," I said, "she left her husband for the boyfriend and the boyfriend dumped her."

"Fucking her was one thing," O'Connor said. "Marrying her was another."

"I guess," I said. "You know the other thing that bothers me, her husband's got the kid."

"She got a kid?"

"Yep."

"And the kid's with the husband."

"Yep."

"Doesn't fit with your usual stalker," O'Connor said.

"Custody of the kid?"

"Yeah."

"No it doesn't. But you never know. He could love his kid and still be crazy."

"I got seven," O'Connor said. "The two may go together."

"You going to stay on this for a while?" I said.

"Yep. We'll keep a car checking her, keep the file open. 'Bout all we can do."

"I'll talk to the ex-husband, and the ex-boyfriend," I said. "I learn anything I'll let you know."

"Thanks," O'Connor said. "You learn who it is you might try dealing with him one to one. We can help her get a restraining order and we can warn him he's subject to arrest. And sometimes if it's done right he can get hurt resisting arrest. But it usually works better if you get his attention before we're involved."

"I'll keep it in mind," I said.

CHAPTER TEN

I got to Lillian Temple's office in the university English department at two o'clock exactly, hoping to impress her with my punctuality. It proved an ineffective approach, because she wasn't there and the office was locked. I leaned on the wall outside her office until ten minutes past two when she hurried down the hall carrying a big blue canvas book bag jammed with stuff. She didn't apologize for being late. She was, after all, a professor, and I was a gumshoe. Apology would have been unbecoming. At first glance I figured that Hawk had called it on her appearance, but when we got seated in her small office and I looked at her a little more, I wasn't so sure.

She was plain, and she was plain in the Cambridge way, in that her plainness seemed a deliberate affectation. Had she chosen to treat her appearance differently, she might have been pretty good-looking. She was in the thirty-five to forty range, tallish, maybe 5'8", brown hair worn long, no makeup, loose-fitting clothes straight from the J. Crew catalog. Large round eyeglasses, quite thick, with undistinguished frames, a mannish white shirt, chino slacks, white ankle socks, and sandals. She wore no jewelry. No nail polish. Her most forceful grooming statement was that she seemed clean.

"May I see some identification, please," she said.

I showed her some. She read it carefully. It was a small office on an interior wall, and it was lined with paperback editions of English lit classics: *The Mill on the Floss, Great Expectations,* case books on English lit classics. Blue exam booklets were stacked in a somewhat unstable pile on a small table behind her chair. Above her desk was a framed diploma from Brandeis University indicating that she had earned a Ph.D. in English language and literature. She wore no perfume, but I could smell her shampoo—maybe Herbal Essence, and the faint odor of bath soap—maybe Irish Spring. I could see the neat part line on the top of her head as she looked down at my credentials.

She looked up finally, and handed me back my identification.

"I've asked the department ombudsman, Professor Maitland, to sit in on this interview," she said.

Ombudsman. Perfect. I looked serious.

"Gee," I said. "Couldn't we just leave the door ajar?"

She suspected I might be kidding her, I think, and she decided that her best course was to look serious too.

"Is Amir Abdullah an English professor?" I said.

She thought about my question and apparently decided that it was not a trap.

"Yes," she said. "African-American literature."

"But he has offices in the Afro-American Center."

"The African-American Center, yes, he prefers to be there."

"And what do you teach?"

"Feminist studies," she said.

"Anybody teaching dead white guys?" I said. "Shakespeare, Melville, guys like that?"

"Guys," she said, "how apt."

I think she was being ironic.

"Apt is my middle name," I said.

She nodded, still serious.

"Traditional courses are offered," she said.

A tall handsome man with a thick moustache walked into the office. He had on a brown Harris tweed jacket with a black silk pocket square, a black turtleneck, polished engineer's boots, and pressed jeans.

"Hi, Lil," he said, "sorry I'm late."

He put out his hand to me.

"You must be the detective," he said. "Bass Maitland."

He had a big round voice.

"Spenser," I said.

We shook hands. Maitland threw one leg over the far corner of Lillian's desk and folded his arms, ready to listen, alert for any improprieties. I restrained myself. Whenever I got involved in anything related to a university, I was reminded of how seriously everyone took everything, particularly themselves, and I had to keep a firm grip on my impulse to make fun.

"I'm here at Lillian's request," he said. "My role here is strictly to observe."

"Open-shuttered and passive," I said.

He smiled.

"How do you feel," I said to Lillian Temple, "about the allegation that Robinson Nevins was responsible for the suicide of Prentice Lamont?"

"What?"

"Do you think Nevins had an affair with Lamont? Do you think that the end of the affair caused Lamont's suicide?"

"I . . . my God . . . how would I . . . ?"

"Wasn't it discussed in the tenure meeting?"

"Yes . . . but . . . I can't talk about the tenure meeting."

"Of course," I said, "but such an allegation would certainly have weighed in your decision. How did you vote?"

"I can't tell you that." She looked shocked.

"You could tell me how you feel about the allegation."

She looked at Maitland. Nothing there. She looked back at me.

"Well," she said.

I waited.

"I feel . . . ," she said, "that . . . each person has a right to his or her sexuality."

"Un huh."

"But that with such a right there is a commensurate responsibility to be a caring partner in the relationship." She stopped, pleased with her statement.

"You think Nevins was a caring partner?"

"Not," she spoke very firmly, "if he left that boy to die."

"And you think he did," I said.

"I suspect that he did."

"Why?"

"I have my reasons."

"What are they?"

She shook her head.

"Oh," I said, "those reasons."

"There's no call for sarcasm," she said.

"The hell there isn't," I said.

"I think that's probably enough, Mr. Spenser," Maitland said.

"It's not enough," I said. "But it's all I can stand."

I stood. Maitland still sat half on the desk, looking bemused and neutral. Lillian Temple sat straight in her swivel chair, both feet flat together on the floor, her hands folded in her lap, looking implacable. I got to my feet.

"I'm sorry I can't help you more," she said. "But I do not take my responsibilities lightly."

"You don't take anything lightly," I said.

As I walked past the African-American Center on my way to the parking lot, I thought that while I had been fiercely bull-shitted in the English department, no one had tried to kick my head off. Which was progress.

CHAPTER ELEVEN

Burton Roth lived in an eight-room white colonial house with green shutters on a cul-de-sac off Commonwealth Avenue in Newton. I went to see him in the late afternoon on a Thursday when he said he'd be home from work a little early. We sat in front of a small clean fireplace in a small den off his small dining room and talked about his former wife.

"She always had that flair," he said. "It made her seem maybe more special than she really was."

"You miss her?" I said.

"Yes. I do. But not as much as I first did. And of course I'm really angry with her."

"Because she left."

"Because she took up with another man, and left me for him, and for crissake she wasn't even smart enough to find a good one."

"What would have constituted a good one?"

"One that loved her back. The minute she was free of me he dumped her."

"You'd have felt better about things if she'd married him?"

"And been happy? Yes. This way she wasted our marriage, for nothing, if you see what I mean."

"I do," I said.

He was a well-set-up man, middle sized with sandy hair and square hands that looked as if he might have worked for a living. On the mantel over the fireplace was a picture of a young girl.

It had the strong coloration of one of those annual school pictures that kids take, but the frame was expensive.

"Your daughter?" I said.

"Yes. Jennifer. She's eleven."

"How's she handling all this," I said.

"She doesn't understand, but she's got a good temperament. She sees her mother usually every week. Divorce is hardly a stigma in her circles, half her friends have divorced parents."

"She's all right?"

"Yes," Roth said, "I think so."

"Where is she now?" I said.

"She has soccer practice until six," Roth said. "I have to pick her up then."

"You dating anyone?" I said.

"I don't mean to be discourteous, but you said you were investigating something about my ex-wife and a stalker."

"Stalking is usually about control or revenge or both. I'm trying to get a sense of whether you are controlling or vengeful."

"My God, you think I might be stalking her?"

"It's a place to start," I said.

Roth was quiet for a time. Then he nodded.

"Yes, of course, who would be the logical suspect?" he said.

"Did you say you were dating?"

"I'm seeing someone," Roth said. "She's fun. We sleep together. I doubt that we'll walk into the sunset."

"Do you think your ex-wife would invent a stalker?"

"Well," he said, "she's pretty crazy these days. So much so that I'm careful about letting Jennifer spend time there. KC and I had a pretty good fight about it, and I can't simply keep her away from her mother. But I always stay home when she's there so she can call me if she needs to."

"So you think she might?" I said.

"No, I don't really. I think she might go out with her boyfriend, now former boyfriend, and leave Jennifer alone. Or I think she might bring her with her when she and the boyfriend went someplace that was inappropriate for an eleven-year-old girl. She might be crazy that way, sort of like in junior high school where there was a girl who was boy crazy. But for all her drama and affect, she is a pretty shrewd woman in many

ways, and I think she loves her daughter, and I don't think she'd
invent a stalker, even to blame me."

"Why would she want to blame you?"

"Because she feels guilty about leaving me, and she feels like
a fool for being in love with a guy who dumps her, and she can't
stand either feeling, so she needs to make it my fault somehow."

"You seeing a shrink?" I said.

"Oh, yeah," Roth said. "This is much too hard to do alone."

"You know the boyfriend?"

"We've never met."

"Know his name?"

"Just his first name, Louis."

"How do you feel about him?"

"I'd like to kill him."

"Of course you would," I said.

"But I won't."

"No," I said.

"You sound like you understand that."

"Yes," I said.

He looked at his watch.

"I've got to pick up my daughter," he said. "I don't want to
discuss this in front of her. Would you like to schedule another
time to talk?"

"Not for the moment," I said. "If I need to, I'll call you."

"I am happy to help with this. I don't want Jennifer's mother
to be stalked."

"Do you still love her?" I said.

"Yes," he said. "But less than I used to and in time I won't."

"Good," I said.

CHAPTER TWELVE

I'd put it off as long as possible. Now I had to talk to Prentice Lamont's parents. It was always the worst thing I did, talking to the parents of a dead person. It almost didn't matter how old the deceased had been, it was the parents that were the hardest. I'd had to do it a couple years ago for the parents of a girl alleged to have been raped and killed by a black man. The mother had called me a nigger lover and ordered me to leave. It often was the mother that was most frenzied. In the case of the Lamonts, it was worse because they were divorced, and I'd have to do it twice.

I started with the mother.

"Yes," she said, "Prentice was gay."

"Do you know if Robinson Nevins was his lover?" I said.

"Well," Mrs. Lamont said. "You get right to it, don't you?"

"There aren't any easy questions here, ma'am, and they don't get easier if I sneak up on them."

"No," she said. "They don't."

She was a smallish dark-haired lively woman, not bad-looking, but sort of worn at the corners, as if life had been wobbly. We sat in the yellow kitchen of her apartment on the first floor of a three-decker off Highland Ave in Somerville.

"So what do you know?" I said. "About Prentice and Robinson Nevins."

She shrugged. The initial horror of her son's death had faded with the six months that had passed. The sadness was deeper and probably permanent. But she was able to talk calmly.

"I think Prentice knew we weren't too comfortable about him being gay. He didn't talk much about it in front of us."

" 'Us' being you and his father?"

"Yes."

"You're divorced."

"Yes. Five years ago."

And she still talked about *us*. Things didn't go away from Mrs. Lamont.

"Did he know Robinson Nevins?"

"I don't know."

"Would he have dated a black man?"

"I shouldn't think so, but I wouldn't have thought he'd be gay either."

"Do you think he killed himself?" I said.

"Everyone says he did."

"Do you believe them?"

I pushed too hard. Her eyes began to fill.

"How can I believe he killed himself?" she said. "And how can I believe someone killed him? Prentice . . ."

"Awful stuff, isn't it," I said.

She nodded. She couldn't speak. The tears were running down her face now.

"I'll find out, Mrs. Lamont, it's all I can offer you. I'll find out and then you'll know."

Still she couldn't speak. Again she nodded her head.

"Would you like me to leave?" I said.

She nodded.

"Are you going to be all right?"

She nodded. There were more questions. But you had to be a tougher guy than I was to ask them now. As far as I knew, there wasn't anyone tougher than I was, so I patted her shoulder uselessly and got up from her kitchen table and left.

THIRTEEN

The old man was a different story.

I met him and his more recent wife for a drink at an athletic club in the financial district. Lamont and his wife were both in workout gear. She carried two small racquets. He was bald, medium sized, muscular, and deeply tanned. She was blonde, medium sized, muscular, and deeply tanned. She was also about the age that his son must have been when he did his Brody. Her name was Laura. We sat by a window looking down at the indoor tennis courts where several games of mixed doubles were progressing badly.

"Whew," Lamont said after we'd shaken hands. "She's starting to push me."

"Oh, not very hard," Laura said.

"Racquetball?" I said.

"Yeah. You play?"

"No," I said.

"Ought to, it's a great workout."

"Sure," I said. "Do you know Robinson Nevins?"

Lamont's eyes narrowed.

"That's the jigaboo was supposed to be involved with my ex-wife's kid."

"Not your kid?"

Lamont shook his head.

"He made his choice," Lamont said.

Laura put her hand on top of his on the table.

"You mean he was gay," I said.

"No need to clean it up with a cute word," Lamont said. "He was a homosexual."

"And his choice was you or homosexuality?"

"I'm an old-fashioned guy," Lamont said. "In my book it's a shameful and corrupt thing for men to have sex with each other. Makes my damned skin crawl."

"I can see that," I said. "So you wouldn't know if he did in fact have a sexual relationship with Robinson Nevins."

"No."

"You ever meet Nevins?"

"No."

"How long have you been divorced from Prentice's mother?" I said.

"Six years."

"When's the last time you saw Prentice."

"When I left the house."

"More than six years?"

"Yes, closer to seven. The divorce took about ten months. Obviously, I wasn't living there while it processed."

"So you hadn't seen your son for what, six, six and a half years before he died?"

"For me," Lamont said, "he died a long time ago."

"Was he an issue in the divorce?"

"Well, if she'd brought him up right, maybe he'd be alive now."

"Maybe," I said. "You have any thoughts on his suicide, any reason to doubt it, any reason to think it might not have been Nevins who triggered it?"

"As I say, Mr. Spenser, for me Prentice died a long time ago."

"I wonder if he'd have lasted longer if he had a father."

"Mr. Spenser!" Laura said.

"That's a cheap shot, pal. You got kids?"

"Not exactly," I said.

"Then you don't know shit."

"Probably don't," I said.

I looked at Laura. "I hope he's a better father to you, ma'am," I said.

I didn't want to scramble his teeth. I wasn't even mad. I was sad. It was all sad. Families breaking up, people dying, mothers grieving.

For what?

I stood and walked away.

For fucking what?

CHAPTER FOURTEEN

Belson and two other detectives had talked to thirty-five people about Prentice Lamont, and twenty-nine of them had been a routine waste of time. Professors Abdullah and Temple had alleged that Lamont had been having a love affair with Robinson Nevins. Though not to me. I wondered why they were so reluctant to speak to me. Academics, being academics, attached great importance to abstraction, and there may have been reasons that had to do with listening long to the music of the spheres, reasons a mind as deeply pedestrian as mine would not be able to understand. I had already talked with his parents. Not very informative and not very pleasant either. Next on the list were Robert Walters and William Ainsworth, who were listed as close friends. They had been associated with Lamont in his pamphleteering career.

The pamphlet was published out of Lamont's apartment and despite his demise it was still appearing. His successors had agreed to meet me there. When I arrived the door was open.

One of the two men said, "Are you Spenser?"

I said, "Yes."

He said, "Come in. We're Walt and Willie. I'm Walt."

I shook hands.

"You can sit on the bed, if you want," Walt said.

"I'd just as soon stand," I said. "That way I can stroll around while we talk, and look for clues."

It was a bed sitting room with a kitchenette and bath. The floor was covered with linoleum. The walls were plasterboard painted white. There were travel posters Scotch taped on the wall; the tape had pulled loose, and the posters curled off the wall like wilting leaves. The bed was covered with a pale blue chenille spread. There was a pine kitchen table in the middle of the room with a kitchen chair in front and a big important-looking computer on it. There was a color monitor on top of the hard drive and a laser printer under the table along with a tangle of lash-up. A recent issue of the publication was piled on the table beside the computer screen. Several open cans of diet Coke were scattered around the room. None of them looked recent.

"This the latest newsletter?" I said.

"Yes."

"Mind if I look at it?"

"No," Walt said, "go ahead."

He was a tall trim man with a smallish head. Hc looked like he exercised. He had even features and short brown hair brushed back and a clipped moustache. Willie was much smaller, and wiggly. His blond hair was worn longish and moussed back over his ears. There was a sort of heightened intensity to his appearance, and I realized he was wearing makeup. I picked up one of the newsletters.

"*OUTrageous*?" I said.

"I made up the name," Willie said.

He sounded like Lauren Bacall.

"Nice," I said.

The newsletter was one of those things that, pre-computer, would have been mimeographed. It was a compendium of gay humor including a number of lesbian jokes, poetry, gay community news, badly executed cartoons, all of which were sexual, many of which I didn't get. There was a section on the back page headed "OUT OUT" in which famous homosexuals through history were listed and where, as I read through it, it appeared that covert gay people were revealed.

"You out people," I said.

"You better believe it," Walt said.

"Do that when Prentice was alive?"

"Absolutely," Walt said. "Prentice started it, we're continuing the newsletter just the way he left it, kind of a memorial to him."

"Are there back issues?"

"Sure," Walt said. "All the way to the beginning."

"Which was?"

"Three, three and half now, years ago. When we all started grad school."

"You been in grad school three and a half years?"

"Un huh," Willie said.

"Lots of people go six, eight, nine years," Walt said. "No hurry."

"Could I see the back files?"

"Certainly," Walt said. "They're in the cellar. You can get them before you go."

"Good," I said.

I was walking around the room. I stopped at the window and looked at it, tapping my thigh with the rolled-up newsletter.

"He went out here," I said.

"Yes," Walt said.

"You see any clues?" Willie said.

"Not yet," I said.

I opened the window. It was swollen and old and warped and a struggle. I forced it open finally, and looked down. Ten stories. I put my hands on the windowsill and leaned out. The window was big enough. It would have been no particular problem to climb out and let myself go. And I was probably bigger than Prentice had been. I turned away from the window and looked back at Walt and Willie.

"Prentice a big guy?"

"No," Walt said.

Willie sort of snickered, or giggled, or both.

"Not very butch?" I said.

"Princess?" Willie said and laughed outright, or giggled outright, or both. "That's what we called him."

"Not very butch," Walt said.

"Do you think he jumped?" I said.

Walt said, "No."

Willie shook his head. His hair was so blond I assumed he colored it.

"Then you think he was, ah, defenestrated?"

Walt said, "Yes."

Willie nodded. The nod shook loose some hair above his right ear and he tucked it back in place with a practiced pat.

"You have any idea who?"

Walt said, "No."

Willie shook his head. His hand went automatically to his head to see that the hair hadn't shaken down again.

"Or why?"

"No."

Shake. Pat the hair in place.

"Was he having an affair with Robinson Nevins?"

"Oh, gawd no," Willie said. "That square little prig. Don't be silly."

I looked at Walt.

"No."

"So you know Professor Nevins."

"He's a damned Tom," Willie said.

"Easy for you to say."

"Yeah, well maybe I'm not black but I know about oppression."

"Most of us have," I said.

"Oh, really? Well, who has oppressed you, Mister Straight White Male?"

"Guy shot me last year," I said.

"That's kind of oppressive," Walt said.

"Well, Robinson Nevins is a traitor to his people," Willie said.

"Who are?"

"Every person of color," Willie said.

"Heavy burden," I said. "He out?"

"Out?"

Walt and Willie said it at the same time.

"Nevins isn't gay," Walt said. "He hasn't got the soul to be gay."

"He's the straightest priss I ever saw," Willie said. "He hire you?"

"Not exactly," I said.

"Then who are you working for?"

"Friend of his father's," I said. "Why are you so sure that Prentice didn't kill himself?"

"He had no reason to," Walt said. "I saw him the morning before it happened. He wasn't depressed. He'd, ah, he'd met somebody the night before and was excited about it."

"A lover?"

"Potentially."

"You know who?"

"No."

"Where?"

"No."

"He out any people who might have resented it?"

"Lot of people who are outed resent it, but it has to be done."

"For the greater good," I said.

"Absolutely," Willie said.

"Anyone that might have been really mad?"

"Not to throw Prentice out a window," Walt said.

"Any to-be-outed that might have wanted to forestall him?"

"Oh, come on," Walt said. "This isn't some cops and robbers movie."

"How'd he find the names of people to out?"

"You go to the gay bars, you hear talk at parties, you talk to your friends, see some big contributors to gay-type charities, you sort of nose around, see what you can find out."

"Investigative reporting," I said.

"Exactly."

"You have a file?"

"A file?"

"Of people you suspect that you may out if you can compile enough gossip?"

Willie's eyes went to the desk and flicked away. I'm not sure he was even aware that they'd moved.

"That's not fair," Walt said. "It's more than gossip."

"You have a file?"

"No."

I went to the desk and opened the center drawer.

"Hey," Walt said. "You got no right to be looking in there."

I paid no attention. And neither Walt nor Willie pressed the issue. I found nothing in the center drawer. The side drawer was locked.

"Open it," I said.

"I have no key," Walt said.

I nodded and went to the window. I leaned on it hard and after a struggle got it closed.

"Prentice about your size?" I said to Willie.

"Un huh."

"Open the window," I said.

"You just closed it."

"Humor me," I said. "Open it."

Willie shrugged expressively and went to the window and pushed. It didn't move. He strained until his small face was red. The window didn't move. Walt watched frowning.

"Let me try," he said.

He was bigger and looked like he worked out some. He couldn't budge it either.

"So what's that prove," Willie said. "That you're macho man?"

Walt shook his head.

"Prentice couldn't have opened that window," Walt said.

"So if he jumped he either got someone to open it for him," I said, "or he waited around until it was open."

"My gawd," Willie said, "he really didn't jump."

"Probably not," I said. "You got a key to that drawer?"

"Sure," Walt said.

CHAPTER FIFTEEN

The drawer contained a long list of names of people being considered for outing. I took it with me and back issues of *OUT-rageous*. It wasn't like Belson to have missed the window. It was probably open when he arrived and he never tried it. I took the stuff back to my office and put it on my desk in a neat pile and looked at the pile. Maybe tomorrow.

I pulled the phone over and called Hall, Peary.

"Louis Vincent, please."

I got switched to his secretary who told me that Mr. Vincent was in a meeting and could he call me back. I said no and hung up. I looked at the pile of material on my desk. I got up and made coffee and drank some. I looked at the pile. I finished my coffee and got up and walked downtown to State Street to see if Louis Vincent was out of his meeting.

He was. But he was on the phone to Tokyo and really couldn't see anybody today without an appointment. His secretary was maybe twenty-three, the kind of athletic-looking young woman who walks to work in her running shoes and sweat socks, carrying her heels in a Coach bag. I tried out one of my specialty smiles—paternal, yet seductive, which is usually very effective with athletic young women. She smiled back. Though she might have been responding to the paternal, and ignoring the seductive. Takes all kinds.

"I can wait," I said.

"Certainly," she said, "though I really can't encourage you."

"That's okay."

I took out one of my business cards, and wrote on the back of it, *KC Roth.* I handed it to the secretary.

"If you'll just give him this, perhaps he'll be able to squeeze me in."

"Worth a try, sir," she said and took my card.

As she went into Vincent's office I noticed that she must have done a lot of work on the StairMaster. I noticed also that she didn't look at the card. In shape *and* discreet was a good combination. She was in there maybe two minutes and when she came out she smiled at me.

"He'll see you in just a moment," she said.

"It's the business card," I said. "It pays to get a quality print job."

She smiled again.

"I'm sure it does," she said.

The office door opened and a man stood in the doorway in full upwardly mobile regalia. He was a tall man who looked like he'd be good at racquet sports. He wore a blue striped shirt with a white collar and a pink bow tie, wide pink suspenders, and the trousers of a dark blue pinstripe suit. His blond hair was longish and combed straight back like Pat Riley's, and his skin had the ruddy look of health and maybe Retin A.

"Spenser? Come on in."

I went in. He must have been churning a lot of accounts. It was a corner office, filled with pictures of family and horses and famous clients, trophies from tennis tournaments, and ribbons from horse shows. His children looked like the kids you see in cereal commercials. His wife looked like a model. The jacket of his blue suit hung on a coat hanger on a coatrack behind the door. There was a pink silk pocket square showing. He gestured me to a seat in front of his desk. The diamonds in his heavy gold cuff links glinted in the understated light from his green shaded desk lamp. He glanced at his watch. A Rolex, how surprising.

"Now how can I help you?" he said.

"Tell me about KC Roth," I said.

"Why do you think I know anything about a person named KC Roth?"

"She told me you were until recently her boyfriend."

He raised his eyebrows and leaned back a little in his chair, and clasped his hands behind his head. Beyond him the view stretched into Boston Harbor and out to the harbor islands. To his left a big color computer screen flickered with the facts of someone's life savings.

"Did she?" he said.

I nodded ingenuously. He leaned back some more.

"By God, you're a big fella, aren't you," he said.

"I try to be modest about it," I said.

"You play some sports?"

"Used to be a fighter," I said. "I'm not sure it was play."

"Ah, the sweet science," he said.

"Sweet science is what happened to my nose," I said. "Were you KC Roth's boyfriend?"

"What is this in regard to?"

"A criminal case."

"Something happen to her?"

"Nothing permanent," I said.

"Well, I . . . I wouldn't want anything to happen to her."

"She's fine," I said. "You were her boyfriend?"

He shrugged and grinned. His teeth gleamed.

"Well, I can count on your discretion?" he said.

"In my business," I said, "you're discreet or you're not in business."

It wasn't really true. I'd blab his name in a minute if I needed to, but there was no point in telling him that. And the answer I gave him sounded like the kind of answer he'd want to believe.

"Yeah, same in my business. You know? You're fucking with people's money, babe, and their hair stands up real stiff."

"So you and KC Roth?"

He grinned, hands still clasped behind his head. He put his feet up on the corner of the desk.

"She could fuck the balls off a brass monkey," he said.

"Good to know."

"Don't misunderstand," he said. "I'm married and plan to stay that way, but, ah, you've seen KC?"

"Un huh."

"So you can see how easy it would be to wander off the reservation one time."

My guess was that he'd been wandering off the reservation since his voice changed.

"Easy," I said.

"Well, I did and I'm not proud of it, but it was a ride."

He winked at me. We knew the score, he and I. Couple of studs. More notches on the weapon than John Wesley Harding.

"Why'd it end?" I said.

"For crissake she left her husband. She wanted me to marry her."

"Don't you hate when that happens," I said.

"You better believe it. I got three kids, big job, my wife's no slouch in the sack either, mind you. KC wanted us to go to Key West and live on the beach."

He laughed. I laughed. Women are so silly. Fortunately there are a lot of them.

"What a ditz," he said. "I told her this isn't about love, KC, this is about fucking. You know what she said? You wanna know?"

"What'd she say?"

"She says, 'What's the difference?' You believe that? What's the difference."

He chuckled. I chuckled too. Man of the world.

"She didn't threaten you when you dumped her?" I said.

"With what?"

"Tell your wife?"

"No. She wouldn't. She's not like that. She's a really sappy broad, but she's not mean. Besides I think she likes the drama. She's all drama. She likes the drama of a clandestine affair, and she likes the drama of a sorrowful breakup, and being heartbroken and all that."

Vincent was a little smarter than he seemed. Or I was as dumb as he was. I too thought that life for KC was a series of dramatic renditions.

"Somebody is stalking her," I said.

"And you're coming to me?"

"Ex-husbands, ex-boyfriends, that's where you usually go," I said.

"Hey pal, I dumped her, you know. I'm not some heartbroken loser sneaking around in the dark. There's plenty more where she came from. Try her husband."

"You replace her yet?" I said.

He grinned at me.

"Like Kleenex," he said. "Use once and discard. There's plenty more."

"Your wife?" I said.

He shrugged.

"She's fine. House in Weston. Kids in private school. Drives a Range Rover. Plays golf. Sex is still good. I'm home at least three nights a week."

"What could be better?" I said.

He nodded enthusiastically. Irony was not his strength.

"It's a pretty good gig," he said. "I gotta admit it. There much money in your line of work?"

"No," I said. "But you meet interesting people."

He stood and put out his hand.

"Nice talking to you."

"You have no thoughts on who might be stalking KC?" I said.

"Knowing KC," he said, "she probably made him up. Have fun."

I nodded.

"Fun's what it's all about," I said.

"And the winner dies broke," he said.

CHAPTER SIXTEEN

Susan and I were walking back to Linnaean Street from the Charles Hotel where we had lunched with her friends Chuck and Janet Olson at Henrietta's Table.

"Your friends are nice," I said.

"Yes, they are."

"As nice as my friends?" I said.

"Like Hawk, say? Or Vinnie Morris?"

"Well, yes."

"Please!" Susan said.

We were on Garden Street walking past the Harvard Police Station. I decided to move the conversation forward, and told her about my encounter with Louis Vincent at Hall, Peary.

"Kleenex?" Susan said. "Women are like Kleenex?"

"Un huh. Use and discard. There's plenty more."

I watched her ears closely to see if any steam escaped. But she was controlled.

"The man is an absolute fucking pig," she said.

"There's that," I said.

"I want him to be the stalker."

"Because he's a pig?"

"Yes."

"Does he fit the profile?"

Susan glared at me for a moment, before she said, "No."

"He appears to be one of the masters of the universe," I said. "Good-looking, well married, good job, lots of dough, endless poon tang on the side. Stalkers are usually losers."

"I know."

"It's usually about control," I said. "Isn't it?"

"Yes."

"I'd guess this guy is in control."

"Not of his libido," Susan said.

"No, maybe not," I said. "On the other hand KC wasn't bopping him under duress."

Susan gave a long sigh.

"No," Susan said, "she wasn't."

"And she didn't dump him, did she?"

Susan thought about that.

"In one sense," she said, "maybe not. She left her husband to marry him. He said, 'I won't marry you.' But who said, 'Therefore it's over'?"

I raised both eyebrows. I could raise one eyebrow, like Brian Donlevy, but I didn't very often, because most people didn't know who Brian Donlevy was, or what I was doing with my face.

"I don't know," I said. "I'll ask."

Susan looked pleased.

"Maybe he could still be the stalker."

"We can always hope," I said.

We reached Linnaean Street and turned right toward Susan's place.

"How about that thing you're doing for Hawk?"

"Well, it is, I believe, turning into a hair ball."

"Oh?"

"I don't think the Lamont kid killed himself."

"Why not?"

I told her how his friends said he was happy and how they were scornful of the possibility that he was having an affair with Robinson Nevins and how the window was hard to open and how Lamont was said to be approximately the size of a dandelion, but not as strong.

"Suicides often appear happy prior to the suicide," Susan said. "They've decided to do it."

"Thus solving all their problems."

"And getting even with whomever they are getting even."

"Which is usually why people do it?"

"Yes," Susan said. "The pathology is often similar, oddly

enough, to the pathology which causes stalking—see what you've made me do is a kind of back door control. It forces emotion from the object of your ambivalence.''

"I don't think he could have opened the window," I said.

"Maybe it was conveniently open when the time came. Maybe its openness was the presenting moment, so to speak.''

"I checked," I said. "It was thirty-six degrees, raining hard, with a strong wind on the day he went out.''

Susan smiled at me.

"So much for psychoanalytic hypothesis," she said.

"It's very helpful," I said. "Especially when you asked about who actually ended KC's affair. But it isn't intended to replace the truth, is it?''

"No. It's intended to get at it.''

We went into Susan's office. Her office and waiting room and what she called her library (it looked remarkably like a spare room with a bath to me) were on the first floor. Her quarters, and Pearl's, were on the second. When Susan opened the door to her living room, Pearl bounded about giving and receiving wet kisses, torn with her passion to greet us both at the same time. But, being a dog, she quickly got over her bifurcating ambivalence and went back and sat on the sofa with her tongue out and looked at us happily.

Susan got me a beer from her refrigerator and poured herself a bracing glass of Evian, and we sat down together at her kitchen counter. Pearl sat on the floor beside us in case we moved into eating.

"So where to now," Susan said.

"One thing is I'll ask KC to go through the breakup, see if he might have experienced it as her leaving him. Second, I figure that Louis has fooled around before.''

"I think you can bank on it," Susan said.

"So I'm going to see if I can find a few former girlfriends and see if there's been any stalking. If he's a wacko, KC can't be the only one he's been a wacko with.''

Susan nodded and sipped some Evian. I drank some beer.

"How about the other case?''

"I've got a stack of back issues of the magazine that Lamont published: *OUTrageous.*''

"As in OUT of the closet?''

"Yes. I'll read through that and see if there's a suspect. I'll look at the plans for future issues, which I also have, and see if there's any suspects there."

"And if there aren't?"

"Then I'll try to establish whether there was or was not a relationship between Nevins and Lamont, and if there was why people didn't know and if there wasn't why people said there was."

"And if that doesn't work?"

"I'll ask you," I said.

"For some psychoanalytic theory?"

"Can't hurt," I said.

"What I think we should do is go take a shower and brush our teeth and lie on my bed and see what kind of theory we can develop."

"I'm pretty sure I know what will develop," I said.

"Should we shower together?" Susan said.

"If we do, things may develop too soon."

"Good point," Susan said. "I'll go first."

"And Pearl?" I said.

"In the living room with the TV on Fox—loud. She loves to watch Catherine Crier."

"Anyone would," I said.

And Susan disappeared into her bedroom.

CHAPTER SEVENTEEN

KC Roth poured some white wine into her glass.

"I was about to have lunch, I could make us both something," she said.

"Thank you, no," I said. "Just a couple questions."

"Did you see him?"

"Vincent?"

She smiled as if I had prayed aloud.

"I saw him," I said. "Handsome devil."

"Oh isn't he," she said. "What did he say?"

"He said he didn't stalk you."

"What else."

She was sitting on the pink sofa in the bay window of her beige living room. I was back in the uncomfortable gray chair.

"Nothing of consequence," I said. "Could you run back over the breakup."

Her eyes filled. She sipped some more white wine.

"I don't think I can," she said.

"Well, let me help you focus. Who said that you would no longer sleep together."

"What difference does it make?" she said. "It's over."

There were tears now on her cheeks. She wiped them with the back of her left hand.

"It might make a difference," I said. "I know it's painful, but think back. Who decided that you'd stop making love."

She drank wine again and looked down at her lap and answered me so softly that I couldn't hear her.

"Excuse me?" I said.

"I did," she said. "I told him that if he wouldn't leave his wife then I wouldn't fuck him until he did."

"Negotiating ploy?" I said.

She looked up and her eyes though teary were harder than one would have thought.

"I was desperate," she said.

"But you meant it."

"Well, he had to lose something too," she said. "He couldn't have everything. I have to leave my beautiful house and my beautiful daughter . . ." Now she was not just teary, now she was crying. "I have to live in this . . . this cell block. He can't keep on fucking me. He has to give up something."

"Fair's fair," I said.

Struggling with her crying she said, "Could you . . . could you come and sit beside me?"

"Sure."

I went and sat on the couch beside her and she leaned over and put her face against my chest and sobbed. I put an arm around her shoulder and patted. Uncle Spenser, tough but oh so gentle. After a while she stopped crying, but she stayed with her face pressed against my chest, and turned a little so she had snuggled in against me.

"So in fact you broke it off," I said. "Not him."

"All he had to do was leave his wife."

"Which he wouldn't."

"He can't. She's too dependent."

"But he'd have been willing to have you as his girlfriend."

"Yes."

"Being the only one cheating in fact didn't bother him."

She shrugged.

"No," she said. "Sometimes I say things because they sound right."

"Most people do," I said.

She seemed to wriggle a little tighter against me, though I didn't see her move.

"You're very understanding," she said.

"Yep."

"And you always seem so clear."

"Clear," I said.

"Have you ever cheated on Susan?"

"Once. Long time ago."

"Really?"

"Yep."

"She ever cheat on you?"

"That would be for her to answer," I said.

"If she did would you care?"

"Yes."

"Did she care the time you did?"

"Yes."

"How'd she find out?"

"I told her."

"Would she have known if you hadn't told her?"

"Maybe not."

"Why did you tell her?"

"Seemed a good idea at the time," I said.

"If you did again would she care?"

"Yes."

"Would you tell her?"

"I'll decide after I do it again."

"Do you think you'll do it again?" she said.

I couldn't figure out how she had moved so much closer to me, since she had started out leaning on me.

"Day at a time," I said.

My voice sounded a little hoarse. She turned her head slightly on my chest so she could look up at me. One hand kneaded my left bicep.

"You're awfully strong, aren't you?"

I cleared my throat.

"It's because my heart is pure," I said.

I was still hoarse. I cleared my throat again. Her face was so close to mine that her lips brushed my face when she spoke.

"Really?"

"Sort of pure," I said.

She raised her head a couple of millimeters and kissed me hard on the mouth. It seemed ungallant to struggle. She pulled her head back.

"When you kiss me put your tongue in my mouth," she said.

Her voice had thickened and grown richer, so that it had acquired the quality of butterscotch sauce. She kissed me again and opened her mouth. I kept my tongue to myself. She pressed harder. I thought that somewhere there must be laughter, as I clung to my chastity. Finally she pulled her head back and looked at me.

"Don't you want to fuck me?" she said.

"Very respectfully, no."

"My God, why not. I know you're aroused."

"You're very desirable," I said. "And I get aroused at green lights."

"Then, what?"

"I'm not at liberty, so to speak."

"My God, you're Victorian. A Victorian prude."

I disagreed, but arguing about my prudishness didn't seem productive. I shrugged.

"It's because of Susan?"

"Sure," I said.

She had sat up and was no longer leaning against me. This was progress, it would help my arteries relax. KC poured some more white wine and drank a swallow.

"What's so great about Susan?"

"The way she wears her hat," I said. "The way she sips her tea."

"Seriously, what's so special about her? I mean I've known her longer than you have, since we were in college. She's so vain, for God's sake."

"I'm not so sure it's vanity," I said.

Better to be talking about Susan than about what to do with my tongue.

"Well, what the hell is it, then. Hair, makeup, clothes, exercise, diet, always has to look perfect."

"Well," I said, "maybe she thinks of her appearance as a work of art in progress, sort of like painting or sculpture."

"And she's so pretentious, for God's sake. She's always like lecturing."

"And maybe not everyone gets it," I said.

"Gets what?"

"Susan's pretty good at irony."

"What's that mean?"

"She understands herself well enough to make fun of herself," I said.

"You'll defend her no matter what I say, won't you?"

"Yep."

KC got up and walked to the other side of the room and stared out the window at the blacktop parking lot behind her building.

"Do you think Louis is the stalker?"

"Could be."

"But why would he?"

"Maybe he feels like he's lost control of you."

"But we love each other."

"Not enough for him to leave his wife," I said. "Not enough for you to sleep with him if he doesn't."

"Of course I won't. Why would I give him what he wants when he won't give me what I want."

"I can't think of a reason," I said.

"Well, I don't believe it. I don't believe a thing you've said about him."

"Just a hypothesis."

"Why isn't my ex a hypothesis?"

"Doesn't seem the type," I said.

"How the hell would you know what type he is?"

"I talked with him."

"And you think that's enough?"

"No, but it's all I've got. I'm not a court of law here. I am allowed to go on my reactions, my guesses, my sense of people."

"And you sense that Louis would stalk me and Burt would not?"

"Yes," I said.

"Well, I don't have to listen to you. And I won't."

"Reading cops still checking on you," I said.

"Like you care."

I stood. "Time to go," I said.

"Past time."

I walked toward the door. She turned slowly to watch me, her hands on her hips, her face flushed.

"I would have shown you things that tight-assed Susie Hirsch doesn't even know."

I smiled at her. "But would you have respected me in the morning?" I said.

"Prude."

"Prudery is its own reward," I said, and left with my head up. I did not run. I walked out the door and toward my car in a perfectly dignified manner.

CHAPTER EIGHTEEN

When I came into my office in the morning there was a message on my answering machine from Prentice Lamont's mother. It had come in late yesterday while I was in KC Roth's condo preserving my virtue.

"Mr. Spenser, Patsy Lamont. I need to see you, please."

I had some coffee to drink and some donuts to eat and the tiresome-looking pile of homosexuals-to-be-outed list still to read. Reading it while eating donuts and drinking coffee would make it go better.

I called Patsy Lamont.

"Spenser," I said. "When would you like to see me?"

She sounded like I'd awakened her, but she rallied.

"Could you come by around noon?" she said. "I have my support group in the morning."

"Anything I can do on the phone?" I said.

"No, I, I need to talk with you."

"Be there at noon," I said and hung up.

I took a bite of donut, a sip of coffee, and picked up the Out list. There were some surprises on it, though none of them seemed like a clue, and by 11:30, with the coffee a dim memory, and the donuts a faint aftertaste, I put the list down and headed for my car. All I could think of was to talk with each of the people on the list. This, coupled with trying to find out who else Louis Vincent had been hustling, meant a great deal of boring legwork that made me think about becoming a poet.

I parked illegally near Mrs. Lamont's three decker and rang

her doorbell at noon. Prudish but punctual. We sat at her thick wooden kitchen table with the high sun shining in through the upper panes of the window over her sink. There was a big white envelope on the table in front of her. It had been mailed and opened.

"Would you like some coffee?" she said. "I have instant."

"No thank you."

"Tea?"

"No ma'am."

"I'm going to have some tea."

"By all means," I said.

I sat at the table with my hands folded on it, like an attentive grammar school student, and looked around. It was a kitchen out of my early childhood: painted yellow, with luan mahogany plywood wainscoting all around, yellow, gray, and maroon stone patterned linoleum on the floor, white porcelain sink, an off-white gas stove with storage drawers along one side. The kitchen table top was covered with the same linoleum that covered the floor. The hot water kettle whistled that it was ready, and Mrs. Lamont poured hot water into a bright flowered teacup. She plopped in a tea bag and brought the teacup in a matching saucer to the table. She took a spoon from a drawer in the table and prodded the tea bag gently until the tea got to be the right shade of amber. Then she took the tea bag out and put it in the saucer. She picked up the teacup with both hands and held it under her nose for a moment as if she were inhaling the vapors. Then she sipped and put the cup back down.

"I barely know you," she said.

"That's true," I said.

"And yet here you are," she said.

"Here I am."

"My husband took care of all the financial things," she said.

I nodded.

"When he left I didn't even know how to write a check."

I nodded again. You find something that works, you go with it.

"I don't know any lawyers or people like that."

I nodded. She had some tea. I waited.

"So when this stuff came in the mail, I didn't know who to ask."

"This stuff?" I said and patted the big envelope.

"Yes. Now that he's . . . gone, his mail comes to me."

I knew who he was. I knew that parents tended to think of their children as *he,* or *she,* or *they,* as if there were no one else that could be so designated. And I knew that when something bad happened to a child the tendency exacerbated.

"Would you like me to look at it?" I said.

"Yes, please."

She handed me the envelope. It was a financial statement from Hall, Peary. Home of that great romantic, Louis Vincent. Boston isn't all that big, sooner or later cases tended to overlap. The statement showed that Prentice Lamont and Patsy Lamont JTWROS had $256,248.29 in a management account consisting mostly of common stocks and options. I copied down the name and phone number of his financial consultant which was listed at the top. It wasn't Louis Vincent. It was someone named Maxwell Morgan.

"What is it?" she said.

"It's a financial statement from a stockbroker."

"What does it say?"

"It says that your son and you had two hundred fifty-six thousand and change invested in stocks and bonds, which the stockbroker managed for him."

"You mean Prentice's money?"

"Yes. Now yours I assume."

"Mine?"

"Yes, see this, JTWROS? Joint tenants with right of survivorship. It means that now that your son has passed away the money is yours."

"Mine?"

"Yes."

"Where would Prentice get two hundred thousand dollars?"

"I was hoping you'd know," I said. "His father?"

She snorted, in a gentle ladylike way.

"You've talked to his father."

"Yes. I withdraw the question."

I picked up the envelope. It was addressed to both Prentice and Patsy at Patsy's address.

"Envelopes like this come here before?"

"Yes. Every month. I just gave them to him."

"He wasn't living here."

"No, he lived in that apartment where they had the newspaper."

But he had the statements sent here.

"What should I do?" Mrs. Lamont said.

"With the money?"

"Yes."

"Do you need it?"

"Need it?"

"It's yours," I said.

"Are you sure?"

"Yes."

"How do I get it?"

"Somewhere in Prentice's effects there's probably a checkbook."

"He showed me one once."

"What'd he say?"

"I don't recall exactly, just something about see this checkbook."

"If you had it you could simply write a check on this account when you needed to."

"Maybe in his room," she said. "It's not the room he grew up in. We lived in Hingham until the divorce. It's just the room he used when he came to see me. A child always needs to have a home to come to."

"Yes," I said.

"I haven't been in his room since the funeral."

"Would you like me to look?"

She was silent, looking into her teacup, then she nodded.

"Yes," she said very softly.

It was a small room behind the kitchen. Single bed with a maple frame and flame shapes carved on the tops of the bedposts. A braided rag rug, mostly blue and red, that was a little raveled at one edge. A patchwork quilt, again mostly blue and red, covering the bed, some jeans and sport shirts and a pair of dark brown penny loafers in the closet. A maple bureau with an assortment of school pictures on top of it. Prentice Lamont when he was in first grade, looking stiff and a little scared in a neat plaid shirt, and in most of the grades between. His high school graduation picture dominated the collection, a round-faced kid with dark hair and pink cheeks, wearing a mortarboard. His bachelor's degree was framed on the wall, but no college graduation picture. In the top drawer of the bureau was a checkbook and a box of spare checks and deposit slips and mailing envelopes. Apparently Prentice did his financial planning in Somerville.

There was nothing else of interest in the room. It wasn't a room that spoke of him, of his sexuality, his fears, why he was dead, or who killed him. It was an anonymous child's room, maintained by a mother, for an adult to come and sleep in once in a while. I brought the checkbook and the spare checks out to his mother.

CHAPTER NINETEEN

Hawk and I were sparring in the boxing room at the Harbor Health Club. There was no ring, just an open space to the left of the body bag and speed bag and the skitter bag that was so hard to nail that even Hawk missed it now and then. We had on the big fat pillow gloves that even if you got nailed wouldn't hurt much, and we were floating like a couple of butterflies and pretending to sting like a couple of bees.

"So, Lamont is outing people," Hawk said.

I put a left jab out and Hawk picked it off with his right glove.

"Un huh."

I turned my head, and rolled back from a right cross and felt the big soft glove just brush past my cheekbone.

"And he got two hundred fifty thousand in his money management account at Hall, Peary."

I tried a flurry of body punches which Hawk took mostly on his elbows, and then closed up on me and clinched.

"Un huh."

We broke and moved in an easy circle around the ring looking for daylight.

"I not a thinker like you," Hawk said, "being the pro-duct of a racist ed-u-cational system."

"This is certainly true," I said and threw a lightning fast left hook which Hawk seemed to catch quite easily on his hunched right shoulder. He countered with a whistling right uppercut which I managed to avoid.

"But if I a thinker," Hawk said. "I be thinking that *OUT* plus money could equal blackmail."

"That's amazing," I said as I circled him clockwise, bouncing on my toes to demonstrate that I wasn't getting tired. "And you're not even a licensed investigator."

Hawk shuffled in suddenly and threw a short flurry of punches which I bobbed and weaved and rolled and ducked and mostly avoided. I countered with an overhead right which Hawk pulled back from. Hawk stepped back and leaned against the wall of the gym.

"You think we go fifteen and not get a winner?" Hawk said.

"Fifteen for real," I said, "maybe we'd be trying harder."

"Have to."

We walked out of the boxing room and down to Henry Cimoli's office.

"How long'd you go," Henry said.

He was in his trainer's costume, a very white tee shirt and white satin sweatpants. His small upper body looked like it might pop the weave in the tee shirt.

"Half hour," I said.

"You need mouth to mouth?"

"Not from you," Hawk said and put his hands out for Henry to unlace the gloves. When we were both glove free, Henry nodded at the small refrigerator next to his desk.

"Trick I learned when I was fighting," he said. "Keep some good sports drinks handy so as to replenish the electrolytes."

I opened the refrigerator and took out two bottles of New Amsterdam Black and Tan.

"You can use my office, you want," Henry said. "I got to go suck around the customers."

"You too teeny to run a health club," Hawk said. "The same people come here year after year, since the place stopped being a dump. Nobody lose weight. Nobody put on muscle. Everybody look just like they did when they signed up to get in shape."

"One difference," Henry said. "They are a little poorer, and I am a lot richer."

Hawk grinned at him.

"Maybe you ain't too teeny after all."

Henry jumped up and kicked the palms of his outstretched

hands with his toes, and landed easily and laughed and went out to the gym floor.

"Agile too," Hawk said.

"Easy to be agile if you're the size of a salt shaker."

"Almost beat Willie Pep once," Hawk said.

"I know."

Hawk sat in Henry's chair and took a pull at the beer. He swiveled the chair so he could look out Henry's picture window at the harbor.

"You getting anywhere on Susan's friend's stalker."

"I got a guy I like for it."

"Time for me to go reason with him?" Hawk said.

"No. I'm not sure he's the one."

Hawk shrugged. He put his feet up on the windowsill and crossed his ankles and took another drink of beer.

"Thing I like about Henry," Hawk said. "He keep the sports drinks cold."

"That's a good thing."

We were quiet for a moment. One of the big harbor cruise boats eased past, all glass and sleek lines, on a luncheon cruise to nowhere. It loomed close to the window. We could see the people, mostly couples, seated at tables in the main cabin.

"You think Robinson connected to the Lamont kid?" Hawk said.

"I don't know yet. I hope not. That thing shows every sign of being a mess."

"See any connection with Abdullah?"

"Nothing you don't know," I said.

The cruise ship had moved out of sight. For a moment the only activity out the window was the wake of the cruise boat and the gulls that swooped ever hopeful behind it. I finished my beer and Hawk reached over without taking his feet down and got two more out of the refrigerator.

"What's going on with Abdullah?" I said.

Hawk didn't move. He continued to look out the window at the harbor. He raised the bottle and took another drink of beer.

"You're completely pragmatic," I said. "You don't care what people call you. You don't care if people are annoying. You don't care about color. You don't get mad, you don't get sentimental. You don't hold a grudge. You don't get scared, or confused, or boisterous, or jealous. You don't hate anyone. You don't love anyone. You don't mind violence. You don't enjoy violence.''

"Kind of like Susan,'' Hawk said.

"Okay,'' I said. "You don't love many. My point stands. You taking a run at Amir Abdullah because he called you a Tom is bullshit. You don't care about insults any more than you care about fruit flies.''

Hawk drank the rest of the beer in his bottle and put the bottle on the desk. He dropped his feet off the windowsill, swiveled around, and got another two bottles out of the refrigerator. He put one on the desk in front of me, opened the other, and leaned back in Henry's chair facing me. His face had no expression. His black eyes were bottomless. I waited. I was barely into my second beer.

"I got you into this,'' Hawk said.

I nodded. One of the water taxis from Logan Airport plodded past. Few couples in this one. Mostly men, a scattering of women. Both genders dressed for business, carrying briefcases, paying no attention to each other, too busy to flirt, or too tired, or it might mess their hair.

"I was about fifteen,'' Hawk said, "making a living as a mugger. Used to go to the Joe Louis gym to use the bathroom. Joe Louis didn't have anything to do with it, of course, but half the black boxing clubs in the country were using his name. Got so I'd hang around in there, watch the fighters. Sometimes when there wasn't much going on they'd let me hit the bag. I figured if I was going to make a living beating people up, I might as well practice. I got good at it. Make the body bag jump, make the speed bag dance. Had trouble in those days with that little jeeter bag, but even some of the fighters had trouble with that.''

"I still have troubles with that,'' I said.

Hawk smiled.

"Naw, you don't,'' he said. "Neither one of us do. So one day Bobby Nevins comes in, sees me working on the bag, asks me have I got a manager? I say no. He says 'You ever fight in the ring?' I say no. So he says, 'You want to try it?' And since I been making a living beating people up I figure why not? So I say sure, and he puts me in with some tall skinny Puerto Rican guy probably don't weigh more than a hundred fifty pounds. And

I'm thinking how smart Bobby is to start me off easy, so I lace 'em on and get in the ring and of course the guy cleans my clock.''

"Knowing how helps," I said.

"It do. But Bobby sees something he likes and he takes me on, and when he finds out I'm not living anywhere special he takes me in, and I learn to fight and maybe along the way to use a fork when I'm eating. Stuff like that. Robinson was a little kid then, maybe twelve, and his mother kept him away from the fighters, so I see him, but I don't know him much. So one day Bobby say to me, 'I think you need to get a little schooling.' And I say why, I gonna reason with people in the ring? And Bobby say, 'You should take an English class and a math class.' And pretty soon I'm in night school at the community college. And my English professor is a brother name of Dennis Crawford. Young guy maybe four, five years older than me. He talk like Walter Cronkite, and he wear horn-rimmed glasses and tweed jackets and English brogues and all around, he about the smartest brother I ever saw. I never saw a black man with an education. Bobby's wife was a schoolteacher, but she didn't spend no time with the fighters so I didn't really know her either, and besides she was a woman. So we reading *Othello* and we reading *Invisible Man* and we discussing them and Professor Crawford, he smarter than the white boys and even the white girls in the class. Never saw nothing like it.''

Hawk tilted the beer bottle back and drank some more and held it up to the light and looked to see how much was left. I stayed quiet. Then he took another swallow and put the bottle down.

"'Course I never say nothing in class. Those days I only know six words if you count mother fucker as two. But I listened. One day after class Professor Crawford asks me to come to his office.''

Hawk had turned so he was staring out at the now empty harbor where the ocean moved in its directionless way.

"When I get there he say he notice me in class and don't think I'm your usual night school student and he ask what I do. And I tell him I'm a fighter and he says well tell me a little about that, so I do.''

I was as still as I was able to be and still breathe. The air in the room seemed to have gotten suddenly very dense. I wanted to drink some beer but I didn't want to move. Hawk swung slowly around and let his feet rest on the floor.

"And while I'm telling him, he hit on me," Hawk said with no discernible change in his voice.

"Shit," I said.

"I got up and left. Never went back to his class again. Never told nobody about it."

"Professor Crawford get caught up in the black power movement?"

"Yeah."

"He change his name?"

"Yeah."

"Amir Abdullah?"

"Yeah."

CHAPTER TWENTY

Susan and I had begun having brunch every Sunday at her home. She'd set the dining room table with flowers in a vase and I'd cook something, and when it was ready, we'd sit in her dining room and eat. Pearl normally joined us. Today I had done huevos rancheros with mild green chilies. We were talking about Hawk.

"Was it because the professor was gay?" Susan said.

"I don't think so," I said.

"Would he have reacted the same way if it had been a female professor that hit on him?"

"No. Femaleness didn't matter the way maleness mattered."

"It was because he was treating Hawk as a means not an end," Susan said.

"Avoiding the obvious wise remark about end . . ." I said.

"Thank you," Susan said.

". . . I think so."

"The most august and accomplished black man Hawk had ever met and he—what would the street term be—dissed him?"

"Something like that," I said.

"And years later he turns up. Do you think he remembered Hawk?"

"I don't know. Hawk's probably not the only kid he ever hit on. Still most people meet Hawk remember him."

"Didn't he go out of his way to be insulting?" Susan said.

"Maybe. I think by nature he's an annoying sonovabitch."

"Predators often resent rejection," Susan said.

I shrugged. Pearl was resting her head on my thigh. I cut off a small bite of the linguiça I had substituted for chorizo, and gave it to her.

"You're just confirming her in her bad habits," Susan said.

"Yes," I said, "I am."

Susan stirred some Equal into her coffee. Pearl heard the spoon click in the cup and left me for a more promising prospect. Susan gave her a small forkful of black beans.

"Talk about bad habits," I said.

"At least I'm teaching her to use flatware," Susan said.

"Important for a dog," I said.

Susan smiled. She put her spoon down and put her chin on her folded hands and looked at me.

"It's very odd," she said. "It's like suddenly discovering Beowulf's childhood."

"I met him about the same time this happened," I said.

"When you were both fighting at the Arena."

"Yes."

"You think he's all right?"

"Hawk?"

"Yes."

"Few people are more all right than Hawk," I said.

"He's very contained."

"Very."

"And he pays a high price for it," Susan said.

"You think?"

"The distance between containment and isolation is not so great," Susan said.

"He's got a lot of women," I said.

"But not one," Susan said.

"I guess that's right," I said.

"You ought to know."

"You think I'm too contained?" I said.

"You have me," Susan said.

"A claim no one else can currently make," I said.

"It makes your containment more flexible," Susan said.

"More fun too," I said.

"You're just saying that because I balled your ears off an hour ago."

"Not just that," I said.

Susan ate some of her food.

"This is very good," she said.

"You deserve it," I said.

"Because I'm deeply insightful?"

"Sure," I said. "And you also balled my ears off about an hour ago."

CHAPTER TWENTY-ONE

I had a couple of ways to go in chasing down Louis Vincent. I could talk to the cops in Hingham where he lived. Or I could talk to people at Hall, Peary where he worked. Hall, Peary was closer, so I called over there and talked with Phyllis Wasserman, the human resources director. She told me that of the five complaints of sexual harassment they'd had in the past year, one involved stalking and remained unsolved. Two others, she said, were much closer to angry disagreement than they were to sexual harassment, and the last two had been resolved by firing the harasser. I asked who was involved in the stalking, and she said she was not at liberty. I asked if she would give my name to the victim and ask her to call me. She said she would.

While I was waiting hopefully, I called the Hingham police. It took a little while but I got to the chief, whose name was Roach. They'd had two stalking complaints in the last year. In one case the stalker had been in violation of a court order, and they had been able to arrest him and urge him to change his ways.

"You give me the name?" I said.

"Not without a good reason," Roach said.

"Well, was the stalker a Hingham resident?"

"No."

"Was he a stockbroker?"

"Hell no."

"Okay," I said. "What about the other one?"

"Never caught the guy."

"But the stalking stopped?"

"Yep. My guess is he found someone else."

"That's my guess too," I said. "Can you give me the name of the victim?"

"Nope."

"Can you give her my name and number, and remind her that I'm trying to help some other woman who's going through what she went through?"

"I can do that," Roach said.

"Thanks."

I hung up and sat. The phone was quiet. I swiveled my chair so I could look out my window at the corner of Berkeley and Boylston. I opened the window so I could listen to the traffic. People were already in summer clothes although we were only about half done with May. There was a Ford Explorer waiting for the light on Boylston Street. The sunroof was open and there was heavy metal music thundering up. As I watched, someone stuck a sign out of the sunroof that said *Brendan Cooney for King*. The light changed. The Explorer moved on, its exuberant sign still deployed. The young are very different than we are, I said to myself. Yes, I responded, they have more time. What if you could be young again and were able to undo the things that were done that made you into the person you would later become. But then who would you be. Would Hawk have been Hawk if he hadn't met Professor Crawford/Abdullah? Maybe this wasn't a useful avenue of inquiry. Maybe I should run over a list of the women I'd slept with and see if I could remember how each of them looked with their clothes off.

I was up to Brenda Loring, who had looked excellent with her clothes off, when the phone rang.

"This is Meredith Teitler," a woman said. "Phyllis Wasserman gave me your number."

"I'm a detective," I said. "I represent a woman who is currently being stalked."

"I understand," Meredith said. "What do you wish to know?"

"You worked at Hall, Peary?"

"Still do," she said.

"You were a stalking victim."

"Yes."

"Is it still a problem?"

"I am no longer being stalked," she said.

"Did you ever identify the stalker?"

"No."

"Did you ever date anyone at Hall, Peary?"

"Yes."

"Who?"

"He wouldn't have been the stalker."

"How can you be sure?"

"Well, he just wouldn't. He was, is very nice."

"Can you give me his name?"

"No, really, I'm happy to help. But I don't wish to make trouble for a man who's guilty of nothing."

"Did you ever date Louis Vincent?" I said.

There was silence.

After a moment I said, "May I take that as a yes?"

"Why did you ask about Louis?"

"He's suspected in a stalking on the North Shore," I said.

Again silence. This time I waited her out.

"Yes," she said finally, "I dated Louis Vincent."

"And what caused you to stop dating?" I said.

"I . . . I went back to my husband," she said. "I had dated Louis while my husband and I were separated."

"How'd he feel about you reuniting with your husband?"

"He was very much for it," she said. "That's why I can't . . ."

"Did he have any thought that you might continue to see each other after you reunited?"

"I . . . well, he did say at one point it would be fun if we could still meet once a week or so and . . . ah . . . be in bed together."

"And you said no."

"I said I didn't see how that would work if I were married again. He said he understood."

"Thank you," I said.

"Will this have to come out?" she said. "I mean my husband and I . . . well, it's working now. I'd hate to drag this thing back up."

"I don't see why it has to be a public thing," I said.

"I don't really believe it was Lou," she said.

"You never know," I said.

Profound.

I hung up and went back to looking out the window, and thinking about nudity. It was late afternoon and I was up to how Susan looked with her clothes off, when the phone rang. It was a guy named Al.

"I'm calling for a woman in Hingham," he said. "You know who I mean?"

"Yes," I said.

"She doesn't want to talk about the stalking thing. But if she can help stop it for some other woman she wants to help. She asked me to call."

"You her husband?"

"Something like that," Al said. "I can answer most of your questions."

"One, really," I said. "She ever date a guy named Louis Vincent?"

"I'll ask her," Al said.

The line was silent for a minute or so, then Al came back on the line.

"Yes," he said.

"Anything she can tell me about him?"

"No."

"Already been discussed?" I said.

"Yes."

"Thank her for me," I said.

"You think this guy Vincent is the stalker?"

"Yes, I do," I said.

"You know where to find him?"

"Yes, I do."

"Where?"

"I think I won't tell you," I said.

"Well, you see him, tell him," Al said. "There's a guy looking for him, big guy, had some fights in his life, likes it, tell him when this guy finds him he's going to yank his fucking head off."

"I'll tell him," I said.

CHAPTER TWENTY-TWO

It was nearly noon. I was at my desk with my feet up reading the to-be-outed list I had acquired from Prentice Lamont's file drawer. It was dated at the top two weeks before Lamont died. The list was several pages long with notations next to various names, which apparently suggested likelihood: "not sure" or "dead giveaway." Some were more graphic: "wrinkle room" or "chicken fucker." Near the bottom of the third page was Robinson Nevins, and the notation "research continues." So there was a connection between Prentice Lamont and Robinson Nevins. There were several names I recognized on the list, but nobody seemed more likely than anybody else to have tossed Prentice out the window. Even the women on the list couldn't be eliminated—Prentice was small, and I knew some lesbian women who might throw me out the window.

I put the list aside and picked up the stack of *OUTrageous* magazines again and began to read. It was not pleasant. Whatever Prentice Lamont had been, he had not been a writer. His literary style was school newspaper gossip prose. It was twenty to two and I was on my third back issue of *OUTrageous,* when I came to an interview with "scholar/activist" Amir Abdullah about the problems he encountered as an African-American man who was also gay. The article added nothing to my understanding of the situation, but it did connect Prentice Lamont, already connected to Robinson Nevins by the *Out* list, to Amir Abdullah. It might mean nothing. They were after all also connected to the same university. It didn't mean Robinson was gay. The *Out* list had been still researching the question. And if Robinson were gay it didn't mean that he had been intimate with Prentice Lamont, and even if he had been, it didn't mean he had thrown Prentice out the window. Still when the same names kept turning up, it sometimes meant something. And when nothing else meant anything, it was a thing to hang on to. The interview between Prentice and Amir could have been the source of the story which Amir had passed on to the tenure committee about a connection between Robinson Nevins and Prentice Lamont. Had Prentice asked Amir about Nevins in the course of the interview? Had Amir suggested Nevins to Prentice in the course of the interview? Could Amir have suggested Nevins for reasons of university politics? Could Amir have embroidered what he learned from Prentice for reasons of university politics? I was pretty sure that worse had been done in the service of university politics. And if any of it were true how did it connect to one of the few facts I had—which was that Prentice Lamont was dead, and he'd died with a quarter of a million dollars in the bank. I thought about the quarter million, which was a relief. Sexuality was a slippery devil. Greed you could get a handle on. Any time there's money in a case, what do you do?

"Follow the money," I said aloud, just as if I were the first person to have thought of that approach.

Even when there's sex in the case too?

There's always sex, what are cases about but sex and money.

"Follow the money," I said again.

I pulled my phone over and called Mrs. Lamont.

"Would you call Maxwell T. Morgan at Hall, Peary," I said, "and tell him that he may discuss your and Prentice's account with me?"

"Why?" she said.

"I'm trying to help you find out how there came to be so much money," I said. It wasn't exactly untrue.

"If you think I should," she said.

"I do," I said, and gave her the phone number and made sure she had it right and got up and went out to see Prentice Lamont's financial advisor at Hall, Peary.

Maxwell Morgan had a smaller office than Louis Vincent, two floors lower and in the middle of the building with a view of another building. He didn't seem to mind. He was a big round blond cheerful healthy-looking guy with pink cheeks.

"Max Morgan," he said. "Come on in."

I sat across his desk from him in a moderately comfortable chair with arms. He had on the uniform—shirtsleeves and suspenders, his coat jacket hung neatly on a hanger on the back of his door.

"Care to invest in American Industry?" Morgan said.

"No."

Morgan grinned. "Okay," he said. "You got a thingamajig that says you're a detective?"

I showed him my license.

"So what do you need?"

"You handled Prentice Lamont's investments."

"Yes."

"Lamont is dead."

"Yes, I know, poor devil killed himself, I understand."

"I don't think so," I said.

"You don't?"

"No, but that's not our issue. What can you tell me about the quarter of a million he has invested with you."

"Not much," Morgan said. "Alive or dead Mr. Lamont is entitled to confidentiality."

"Did Mrs. Lamont call you?"

Morgan smiled and nodded. "Just wanted to be sure it was you," he said.

"I understand," I said. "Lawyers."

"You better believe it, the bastards took over Wall Street about five years ago." Morgan shook his head sadly. "This business used to be fun," he said.

"So," I said. "Tell me about all this money that a twenty-three-year-old graduate student suddenly began investing in a management account."

He swiveled his chair sideways and brought the file up on his computer.

"Cash," he said. "Always in the amount of nine thousand."

"Cash?"

"Well, bank checks."

"Close enough," I said. "What bank?"

"Endicott Trust," Morgan said. "You don't think he was a suicide?"

"No," I said. "I think he was murdered."

"Jesus," Morgan said.

"Always the same bank?"

"Yes."

"Always nine thousand dollars?"

"Yes."

"Sounds like he was avoiding the cash reporting laws."

"It does," Morgan said.

"Would he have paid cash for the bank check?"

"Probably. I can call over there for you."

"I'd appreciate it."

While he called, I looked out the window of his office and into the window of the office across from his. There was a guy in shirtsleeves and suspenders on the phone and another guy looking out the window at me looking out the window at him. Was there a guy in shirtsleeves and suspenders talking on the phone on the other side of the building while another guy stared out the window at a guy in shirtsleeves . . . I shook my head and turned back to Morgan.

"Thank you, Bricky," he said. "I owe you lunch."

He hung up and turned to me.

"Cash money," Morgan said. "In hundreds, ninety of them. Several times a week. Each time he'd get a bank check made out to him."

"How often did he deposit with you?"

Morgan looked at his screen for a few moments.

"Averaged about twice a month."

"So what did he do with the rest?"

"Wine, women, and song?" Morgan said.

"Probably not women," I said.

Morgan shrugged.

"Cigarettes, whiskey, and wild, wild men?" he said.

"I don't know," I said. "If he was going to spend it, why did he convert it to bank checks?"

"Maybe put it in his checking account."

"Why not just deposit the cash?" I said.

Morgan shrugged.

"Hey, I'm a simple stockbroker," he said. "You're the fucking sleuth."

"Thanks for reminding me," I said. "Sometimes it's hard to tell."

CHAPTER
TWENTY-THREE

When I got back from Hall, Peary, KC Roth was waiting in the hall outside my office door wearing an ethereal-looking white summer dress. She appeared not to be wearing stockings. Her legs were tanned. She had on white high heels with no back. Even in the harsh fluorescent light she looked like a slumming angel.

"We must talk," she said.

I unlocked my door. KC preceded me into the office. As soon as the door closed behind us, KC turned and pressed herself against me and put her arms around my neck and kissed me urgently.

"Kiss me back," she murmured.

After a while she moved her mouth away and whispered, "Hold me."

She moved her body against mine in several different directions. I had never figured out how women did that. On the other hand I'd never actually hugged a man. Maybe they did it too and I didn't know it.

"I've wanted you since I saw you," KC whispered.

"Don't blame you," I muttered.

"Put your hands on me."

"They are on you."

"They're on my shoulders," KC said.

"It's a start," I said.

She pushed against me more insistently. I would have said more insistent was not possible, but she managed. She bent her head back and looked up at me, and her lips brushed mine as she spoke.

"Have you ever made love in this office?" she said.

"No," I said, "I was waiting to get a couch."

"You could take me now, here, on the floor."

"I think we've gone through this," I said.

"Come on, you want to."

"Of course I want to," I said. "But I'm not going to."

"You have to," she said. "You have to."

"You left your husband for a guy and didn't end up with the guy," I said. "You're being stalked. You're feeling shaky. You need affirmation, and here I am, the guy who's going to rescue you from the stalker."

"That's just talk," she said. "You're a man and I'm a woman."

There wasn't much room to maneuver around that, so I left it alone. I didn't have a lot of experience fighting for my virtue.

"You ever fuck Susan here?" she said, her face almost touching mine.

"I'm impressed," I said. "The question is intrusive, annoying, coarse, and voyeuristic, that's quite a lot to get into a simple question."

"Well, did you? I'll bet you didn't. I'll bet she wouldn't. She wouldn't want to do it in a chair," KC's voice got very flutey, "because it wouldn't be ladylike. And she wouldn't want to do it on the floor because she'd be afraid she'd mess her clothes."

"Enough," I said.

I took a somewhat firmer grip on her shoulders and walked her backward toward one of my client chairs. She thought I was succumbing. I could feel her shoulders relax. I sat her down in my client chair and held her there. She raised her face with her eyes closed and her mouth open.

"You and I are not going to have sex," I said. "I don't like that much better than you do, but it's a fact."

She reached out and began to rub my thigh. I slapped her hand. The action was involuntary, but effective. She pulled her hand away and burst into tears. I went around my desk feeling completely idiotic and sat down, and breathed in and out as quietly as I could. She cried for a little while and rubbed her hand where I'd slapped it.

"You hit me," she said.

"Not very hard," I said.

"It was too hard," she said.

"Hard is in the eye of the beholder, I guess," I said, and wished I hadn't said it quite that way.

KC rubbed her hand some more, and sniveled a little. It didn't seem to me like a good time to tell her that Louis Vincent was almost certainly the guy who was stalking her. Or that she was but one of a fairly long list of women he stalked. Perhaps there was another way to approach that problem.

Then she said, "I don't understand you, most men would jump at the chance to fuck me."

"Of course they would."

"Don't you think I'm beautiful?" KC said.

"Absolutely," I said.

"As beautiful as poopie old Susan?"

"No less," I said.

"You're not even married to her."

"I know," I said.

"I need a man to hold me."

"Maybe you just want one and think it's need."

"What's that mean?"

I shrugged.

"Just a thing to say."

"Well, I've been through hell," KC said with a breathy sorrowful catch in her voice.

I nodded.

"And I don't need a lot of holy-than-thou crap from some guy I've hired."

"I think that's holier," I said, "holier than thou."

"And don't patronize me."

Lucky I was a liberated guy and perfectly correct in my sexual attitudes or I might have said something under my breath about women.

"KC," I said. "I'm trying, with some difficulty, and against most of my genetic programming, to avoid sex with you in a pleasant fashion. Maybe it can't be done. Maybe the closest I can get to it is to patronize you."

She sat and looked at me and thought about that. She was

gorgeous. I knew virtue was its own reward, but sometimes I wondered if the same might be true of vice.

"So tell me about Susan," she said. "What is it she does to make you like this?"

"It has to do with love, I think."

"But how does she get you to do what she wants?"

"She doesn't," I said. "I want to do what she wants."

"But she must do something."

"What she does," I said, "is she tries not to want me to do things I don't want to do."

"I'm serious," KC said.

"Me too," I said.

KC stared at me, she crossed her bare legs and stared some more. Finally she said, "I don't get it."

"No," I said. "You don't."

CHAPTER
TWENTY-FOUR

I took a rosewood-paneled elevator up to the top floors of the State Street Building where Hall, Peary flourished. There were five guys in striped shirts and red suspenders riding up with me. For a guy who kept all his money in his wallet, I was spending a lot of time with stockbrokers. When I went into Louis Vincent's big corner office I closed the door behind me. Louis was contemplating his computer screen, breathless with adoration.

"Hello there," I said. Spenser, the genial gumshoe.

Vincent looked up.

"Oh, hi. Come on in, or, well, you are in, aren't you."

"I bring you greetings," I said, "from KC Roth, and Meredith Teitler, and a woman in Hingham whose name I do not know, but whose significant other is a large fierce man named Al who says he will remove your head if he ever encounters you."

"What the hell are you talking about?" Vincent said.

"Don't dick around with this, Vincent. You've stalked a number of women in the past and you are stalking KC Roth currently."

He got to his feet.

"You're crazy," he said.

I walked around the corner of his desk and put a good short left hook in under his rib cage on the right side. He gasped and staggered back, and began flailing at me with both hands. He was so inept that his fists weren't fully closed and if he'd hit me it would have been more of a slap than anything else. But he didn't hit me. It had been a long time since somebody who punched like he did had hit me. I hit him again, same punch, same place, and he gasped again.

Then he hollered, "Betty."

I punched him in the solar plexus with my right hand and he sagged. He tried to yell Betty again but he had too little breath. Behind me the door opened.

A woman's voice said, "My God."

"Call cops," Vincent gasped.

I stepped away. He tried to straighten up, still struggling to get air in, and I clipped him on the jaw with a good professional right cross and he sat down hard on the floor and stayed there.

"Stop it," Betty screamed, "stop it."

"Done," I said.

Betty turned and ran toward her desk. Vincent was staring at me from the floor. He was about half functional.

"Can you understand me?" I said.

He nodded.

"If anything even slightly annoying, anything at all happens to KC Roth, ever again, I will come back and knock every tooth out of your head."

He continued to stare.

"And maybe I'll tell Al where you are." I could see that he heard me.

"You understand that?" I said.

He nodded very slightly. He was very pale, and he kept himself rigid as if any movement would make him disintegrate.

"Feel free to explain to the cops why I punched you," I said and turned and walked out of his office.

Betty had hung up the phone. When she saw me she pointed me out to a couple of vigorous-looking young guys who were probably good at squash.

"That's him," she said. "Don't let him get away."

I didn't feel like instructing them in the difference between scuffling and squash, so I smiled at them courteously and opened my coat so they could see that I was wearing a gun.

"Let him get away," I said.

Which they did.

CHAPTER TWENTY-FIVE

Pearl and Susan and I were sitting in Susan's large black Explorer in the parking lot of the Dunkin' Donuts shop on Route 1 in Saugus, eating donuts. Actually Susan and Pearl were sharing a donut and I was eating several, with coffee.

"I got a call from KC Roth this morning," Susan said.

She sprinkled a little Equal into her decaffeinated coffee and swirled it with the little red swizzle that came with the coffee.

"Swell," I said.

I liked the donuts they sold with the little handle on them. When you had finished the donut you still could eat the little handle and have the illusion that you'd gotten extra.

"She says you've been hitting on her."

I finished my donut and drank some coffee to help it down.

"And how did you respond?" I said.

"I said that it seemed very unlike you."

"And she said?"

"That apparently I didn't know you as well as I thought I did."

"Well," I said, "if I were going to hit on someone besides you, she'd be an early candidate."

"Yes, she is undeniably stunning," Susan said. "But I'm pretty sure that I do know you as well as I think I do."

"Maybe better," I said.

"So I don't want you to deny it," Susan said. "Because I don't believe you did it. But I'd be curious as to why she is telling me you did."

"She blandished me and I was unresponsive," I said.

"Blandished?"

"Yes."

"As in blandishments?"

"Yes."

"Are you sure that's a word?"

"It is now," I said.

"Tell me about her blandishments," Susan said.

So I did, graphically.

"I don't wish to hurt your feelings, but KC has always been something of a hot pants."

"Damn," I said, "I thought maybe you had told her what a Roscoe I was in bed."

Susan shook her head and sipped some more decaf. "Your secret is safe with me," she said.

From the backseat Pearl nudged at my elbow as I was about to bite into a new donut.

"Excuse me," I said and broke off a piece and gave it to her.

"KC and I have been friends a long time," Susan said. "I would have hoped for a little better behavior."

"Maybe she's different with men than she is with other women," I said.

"I'd say that was a given," Susan said.

"I don't know why, and obviously I'm making some rather large intuitive leaps here, but she seems to be in bad need of male attention and she seems to need it from men she can be scornful of."

"Including you?" Susan said.

"If I had, ah, come across," I said. "Then she could have been scornful of me because I was unfaithful to you."

"Maybe that was part of your attraction, in addition to being a Roscoe, of course."

"This is your department," I said, "but maybe it's why she cheated on her husband. He seemed hard to scorn."

"Yes, Burt is quite admirable. How about her stockbroker?"

"Easy to scorn."

"I of course understand some of that."

"You understand some of everything," I said.

Susan smiled and held her decaf up so Pearl could lap a little from the cup.

"Yes we do," she said. "How did your talk go with Louis Vincent? Did he admit it?"

"Not exactly."

"Did he seem remorseful?" Susan said.

"I think by the end of the discussion he felt some remorse."

"Does his remorse have any connection with the bruised knuckles on your right hand?"

"It was a talking point," I said.

"Did you have to talk much?"

"Awhile," I said.

"So how come there aren't any other bruises on your knuckles."

"All the other talking was to the body," I said.

"Did you reach an agreement?"

"We agreed that he would stop bothering KC."

"Leaving KC all the free time she needs," Susan said, "to bother you."

"Exactly."

"Maybe I'll talk with her."

"And say what?"

"And say that if she doesn't stop fucking around with my honey bun, she'll be sleeping with the fishes."

"You shrinks know just the right thing," I said.

"Yes," Susan said. "We do."

CHAPTER TWENTY-SIX

One of the people who'd been outed by *OUTrageous* was a television reporter named Rich Randolph. I sat with him in his cubby inside the newsroom at Channel Three, next door to the news set.

"I wasn't exactly in the closet," he said. "But I wasn't, you could say, broadcasting it."

"Probably not the road to advancement," I said.

Randolph was slimmer than he looked on camera, with a good haircut, round, gold-rimmed glasses, and a sharp-edged face.

"Hell, glasses put you at a disadvantage."

"And well they should," I said.

He glanced at me for a moment and then smiled.

"Nothing," he said, "is too trivial for local television."

"Did you know Prentice Lamont?" I said.

"He the guy ran the magazine?"

"Yes."

"No, I didn't know him. I saw his name on the masthead. Somebody, I assume it was he, wrote me an unsigned letter saying that I was scheduled to be outed in the whatever date issue of *OUTrageous,* unless I wished to make other arrangements, and included a phone number. I called the number and I said what sort of arrangements, and he said, financial. And I said you mean you'll take money not to out me? And he said, yes, and I told him to go fuck himself, and hung up. About two weeks later I was out."

"Sounds like you passed on a good piece of investigative reporting."

"I did," Randolph said. "It was also my life, and I thought maybe I can just sit tight and it'll blow over. I mean who ever heard of *OUTrageous,* anyway? I thought they might be bluffing, and if they weren't I thought no one read the damned thing."

"Unless they backed it up," I said, "and made sure somebody saw it."

"The station manager got a copy in the mail."

"How'd that work out?"

"He was hurt," he said, "that I hadn't leveled with him. The sonovabitch. Like he's telling me about his sex life."

"But he didn't fire you."

"Hell no. The union would be on them like ugly on a warthog. The PR fallout would swamp him, and he knows it."

"He taking any action?" I said.

Randolph shrugged. "You watch the news on this station?"

"No," I said.

"Well, if you did, you might next see me covering a fashion show."

"Or modeling them," I said.

"Ah, if only," Randolph said.

"Was it Lamont that was doing the blackmail, you think?"

"I don't know. The letter was unsigned, appeared to be written on a computer. The voice on the phone was anonymous. I have no idea who I talked to, but how big an operation was it?"

"Maybe bigger than I thought," I said. "Could you tell anything from the voice? It was male."

"Yeah, male. Native English speaker, I'd say."

"How old?"

"Couldn't tell. Wasn't a kid, or an old person. Twenty to sixty, somewhere in there, I guess."

"Race?"

Randolph shook his head.

"Anything to indicate that it wasn't Prentice Lamont?"

"Given that I don't know who Prentice Lamont is, no."

We sat for a moment. Outside his cubicle the newsroom clattered and hustled. Monitors gleamed. Assignments were being given. Phones were ringing. Computers were being keyed.

"You talk to any other people who've been featured in *OUT-rageous*?" I said.

"No."

I nodded.

"How come you get a cubicle?" I said.

"Senior correspondent," he said.

"Wow," I said.

"Yeah," Randolph said.

We sat for another moment.

"You know what my real name is?" Randolph said. "My real name is Dick Horvitz. Media consultant said it didn't have sympathetic overtones."

"Gee," I said, "I choked up the minute you said it."

"You ever wonder why people care about shit like this?" he said.

"Often," I said.

"You have an answer?"

"No."

He leaned back and put his feet up.

"Senior correspondent," he said.

CHAPTER TWENTY-SEVEN

It was time to find out more about Prentice Lamont. So I drove over to the university and parked my car in a space marked *faculty only*. Actually it was past time to find out about Prentice. If I knew any less I'd be in some sort of informational deficit.

I started with the Dean of Arts and Sciences, whose name was Reynolds. We sat in his first-floor office with a view of coeds in the student quadrangle. His desk was neat without being barren, and a picture of his wife and three daughters was displayed on a side table.

"I can get you Prentice Lamont's transcript," he said, "hold on."

He stood and walked to the door and stuck his head out and spoke to one of the women in the outer office.

Back behind his desk, he smiled.

"Things move quicker," he said, "when it's a request from the dean's office."

Reynolds was a tall trim man with a bald head and horn-rimmed glasses. He wore a dark suit with a red silk tie, and a matching pocket square.

"The information from the English department tenure committee will be harder. Requests from the dean don't impress them, and legally, they have the right to keep their proceedings secret."

"Legally in a court of law?"

Reynolds shrugged.

"I don't know. Legally under university bylaws."

"Even if the proceedings may in themselves have violated university bylaws?"

Reynolds smiled again.

"My guess would be," he said, "especially then."

"Did you know Prentice Lamont?" I said.

"No."

"How about Robinson Nevins?"

"I recognized him if we passed in the corridor, I don't think we've ever talked."

"How about Amir Abdullah."

Reynolds leaned back in his chair and put his hands behind his head.

"Ah," he said, "Mr. Abdullah."

I waited.

"I understand you've already had an altercation with Mr. Abdullah."

"I prefer to say I've already won an altercation with Mr. Abdullah."

"Not everyone can claim that," Reynolds said. "You appear to have the build for it."

"How've you done?" I said.

"Our altercations are somewhat different," Reynolds said. "But I guess we're about even."

"What can you tell me about him?"

"Officially? Professor Abdullah is an esteemed member of our faculty."

"And unofficially?"

"A great pain in the ass," Reynolds said.

"I need to know as much as I can," I said.

"About Abdullah?"

"About everything. You seem to know about Abdullah."

"I know something about Abdullah, and I have some opinions, but they are not for dissemination."

"It is not in the best interest of a guy who does what I do," I said, "to blab things told him in confidence. And you have my word that it will be in confidence unless I am legally compelled to repeat it."

"Fair enough," Reynolds said. "Abdullah is a poseur. He is intellectually dishonest. He exploits his blackness and his gayness for his own advantage. He cares only about his own advancement. He does not like to teach, and his publications are polemic rather than scholarship. He is, I believe, though I've not been able to catch him, a sexual predator who preys on young men in his classes."

"If you catch him?"

"If I catch him," Reynolds said, "he's gone. Tenure or no tenure."

"And you win," I said.

"And I win."

A tall good-looking black woman with gray highlights in her short hair came in carrying a copy of the transcript.

"Who gets this?" she said.

Reynolds pointed at me and she handed it to me and smiled and walked out. I gave the transcript a fast eyeball.

"Prentice took three courses last semester in African-American studies," I said. "Could they be Abdullah?"

Reynolds put out a hand and I gave him the transcript; he glanced through it.

"All of them," he said, "would be Professor Abdullah."

"What is Prentice's major?"

Reynolds glanced at the transcript.

"He was getting a master's degree in English literature," he said.

"Is it unusual that he'd take all these African courses?"

"Yes."

"What department does Abdullah belong to?" I said.

"English. The African-American Center is not funded by the university and has no official standing, though we are not opposed to it, and would be hesitant to oppose it anyway."

"If you do find that he is hitting on young men in his class and you fire him, will there be a firestorm of protest alleging you are homophobic and racist?"

"Absolutely," Reynolds said.

"But you'll do it anyway."

"There are no university bylaws that tolerate sexual exploitation of students by faculty, straight or gay, black or white."

"I can prove he hit on a student at the community college some years ago."

"Doesn't help me here," Reynolds said.

"Maybe it will," I said.

Reynolds studied me for a moment. His eyes were both humorous and hard, like a turtle's.

"One entry," he said after a moment, "into the proceedings of the tenure committee would be to talk with the members. Some are fools, but one or two are quite human."

"Who would you say is the most human?"

"Tommy Harmon."

"Does he know all the words of 'Hail to the Victor'?" I said.

"It's a nickname, I believe his real name is David."

"Doesn't sound like you had to sort through a long list," I said. "To come up with him."

Reynolds smiled.

"I'll call Tommy if you like and tell him you'll be stopping by."

"Do," I said.

CHAPTER

TWENTY-EIGHT

Tommy Harmon had an office with a big bay window that gave him a sweeping vista of the MBTA station. There was a boom box on top of his bookcase and he had a CD playing.

"Carol Sloane," I said.

"With Clark Terry," he said. "Very good."

He was a blocky man with a thick neck and a kind of healthy-looking redness to his face that suggested he spent time out of doors.

"I represent Robinson Nevins," I said.

Harmon nodded.

"He thinks he was jobbed on his tenure promotion."

"I do too," Harmon said.

"And he asked me to look into how that happened."

"And?"

"In the process I came to the conclusion that Prentice Lamont didn't commit suicide," I said.

"You think he was killed?"

"Yes."

"Christ!"

"Which lends a larger urgency to the inquiry," I said.

"I should say so."

"It's my impression that Nevins was denied tenure because of allegations that his relationship with Lamont resulted in Lamont's suicide."

"Nobody ever said that, exactly," Harmon said. "And, of

course, no one is required to explain or even admit their vote. What makes you think he was killed?''

"He couldn't have opened the window he went through," I said.

"Perhaps it was open."

"Perhaps."

"And perhaps I ought to stick to my area of expertise," Harmon said. "Have you shared your theory with the police?"

"Not yet, one of my goals is to refurbish Nevins' reputation, which I thought I might attempt, before I called the cops."

Harmon nodded again.

"What do you need from me?"

"I don't know," I said. "I'd like you to tell me whatever you can about the deliberations of the tenure committee. Maybe I'll recognize something I need."

Harmon reached over and turned off his boom box, then he shifted back in his chair and put one foot up on a partly open drawer in his desk. He was wearing an open-collared white shirt, khaki pants, and white sneakers. On his desk next to a couple of books by R. W. B. Lewis was a book titled *Death in the Landscape: The American Pastoral Vision* by David T. Harmon.

Harmon took in a long slow breath and let it out slowly.

"University politics is very odd. You get a lot of people gathered together who, if they couldn't do this, really couldn't do anything. They are given to think that they are both intelligent and important because they have Ph.D.s and most people don't. Often, though not always, the Ph.D. does indicate mastery over a subject. But that's all it indicates, and, unfortunately, many people with Ph.D.s think it covers a wider area than it does. They think it empowers their superior insight into government and foreign policy and race relations and such. In addition these people are put into an environment where daily, they judge themselves against a standard set by eighteen- or twenty-year-old kids who know little if anything about the subject matter in which their professors are expert."

"Makes it hard not to take yourself very seriously," I said.

"Hard, not impossible," Harmon said. "More of them ought to be able to do it."

"But they can't?"

"But they don't. Exemplar of the species is Lillian Temple.

There is no liberal agenda, however goofy, that will not attract her attention. There is no hypocrisy, however bald, that she will not endure if she can convince herself that it is in the service of right thinking.''

"How about Bass Maitland?" I said.

"Officially he is as committed to right thinking as Lillian," Harmon said. "In fact he is his agenda.''

"He a friend of Lillian Temple?''

"I believe they are more than friends.''

"Lovers?''

"I'd say so.''

"Are they the source of the Robinson Nevins–Prentice Lamont rumor?''

"Yes.''

"Where was Amir Abdullah in this?''

"Amir declines to attend tenure meetings which he views, with some justice, as a bunch of white straight people who will only vote for people like themselves.''

"A situation his attendance might help to modify," I said.

"Amir is never that lucid," Harmon said.

"Is he friends with Temple or Maitland?''

"Since he is gay and black, Lillian feels obligated to like and admire him. Bass tries to, but I believe that Amir makes him uncomfortable.''

"How do you feel about Amir?''

"I think he's a jerk," Harmon said.

"Since Robinson Nevins is black and alleged to be gay, why doesn't Lillian Temple feel obligated to like and admire him?''

"Because he is a relatively conservative black. Which completely confuses Lillian.''

"Harder to feel the white person's burden," I said, "if he's not asking for help.''

"Exactly," Harmon said. "Basically, Robinson is interested in his students and his scholarship, but if asked he will tell you that he is opposed to affirmative action. I have heard him argue that a course, say, in Black Rage, is not an adequate substitute for a course in, say, Shakespeare, or American transcendentalists.''

"Do you share his view?''

"Pretty much. But whether I did or didn't I could still pay

attention to Robinson because he tries to base his views on what he has seen and experienced, rather than on a set of reactions preordained by race or social class. Lillian and maybe Bass, and maybe Amir, though I frankly don't know what makes Amir tick, seem to feel that this is behavior unbecoming a black man.''

"Kind of rattles their stereotypes," I said.

"Yes, I'm afraid it does."

"Would they lie about Robinson to deny him tenure?"

Harmon thought about that. While he thought about it, I looked past him out through his window at an MBTA train grinding out of the station, full of people, mostly students, the train running on elevated tracks for a while to clear the parking lot below it before it dipped with angular sinuosity and disappeared into its tunnel.

"Bass would lie, I think, about anything at all if it served his best interest. Lillian probably would not knowingly lie. She would have to be able to convince herself that it wasn't a lie. Which she could do quite easily, since her grip on truth and falsehood is pretty shaky anyway."

"Who actually told the thing about Robinson?"

"Lillian."

"Did she say where she got it?"

"No."

"How many people believed her?"

"That I can't tell you," Harmon said. "I can tell you that on an eighteen-member committee, Robinson got only three votes for tenure. Mine was one of them."

"Will your colleagues be angry with you for talking so freely?" I said.

"I imagine."

"I can avoid mentioning your name."

"Feel free to mention it. If I said it, I'm responsible for it."

"Okay," I said. "You ever play halfback at Michigan?"

"Tommy's a pretty standard nickname for kids named Harmon," he said. "I went to Williams College. I was a wrestler."

"Ah," I said. "That explains the neck."

"And you used to box," he said.

"Which explains the nose," I said.

"And the scar tissue," Harmon said. "You going to talk with Lillian again?"

"Have to," I said. "I need to know where she got her information."

"I'd like to know where she gets most of it," Harmon said.

We shook hands and I left.

CHAPTER TWENTY-NINE

Lee Farrell and I were drinking beer at a bar called The Limerick, near Broad Street.

"I figured you'd order a pink lady," I said.

"I'm trying to pass," Farrell said.

"It's not working," I said.

"Maybe if I wore my gun outside my coat," Farrell said.

"Might help," I said. "Long as it's not color-coordinated."

"Department issue drab," Farrell said. "My off-duty gun is chartreuse."

"Zowie."

"Yeah. You invite me out to exercise your homophobia, or was there something you needed?"

"Mostly the homophobia," I said. "But have you ever heard of a publication called *OUTrageous*?"

"Yes, I have."

"What do you know about it?"

"It is an obscure journal published by some graduate students which outs prominent gay people."

"You're safe then," I said.

"I'm also out."

"Oh yeah. Is the paper legitimate?"

"I haven't been able to prove that it isn't," Farrell said. "But its editor committed suicide a while ago."

"I know. It's the case I'm on."

"Someone thinks it wasn't suicide?"

"Me," I said.

"So tell me."

I told him why I thought it was murder.

"For obvious reasons, I catch most of the gay squeals," Farrell said. "If you'll pardon the expression. I caught this one. So as soon as you got something that won't give giggle fits to an assistant DA, let me know."

The bartender came down the bar and put a fresh bowl of peanuts in front of us. While he was handy, we ordered two more beers.

"You think there was something wrong with *OUTrageous*?" I said.

"Nothing I can prove," Farrell said.

"But?"

"But there's some blackmail involved."

"There is," I said.

"Got anyone that will testify to it?"

"No."

"We don't either," Farrell said.

"So, what's your take on 'outing'?" I said.

"You start treating people as the means to an end, it's a slippery slope."

"That's what I think. You sure you're gay?"

"Gayer than laughter," Farrell said.

"And younger than springtime."

"You could of got all this from Belson, or Quirk," Farrell said. "Probably did. The gay aspects of this case bothering you?"

"It's a pleasure to watch the work of a trained investigator," I said.

"Yeah, cops are us. What's bothering you?"

I told him about the case.

When I finished, he said, "Guy made a move on Hawk?"

"When Hawk was a kid," I said.

"I didn't know Hawk was ever a kid," Farrell said.

"I knew him when he was a kid," I said. "And I find it hard to imagine."

"You and Hawk were kids together?"

"We fought on the same card when we were eighteen. But Hawk isn't what's bothering me."

"You straight guys are simple tools," Farrell said. "Lemme

tell you what's bothering you. You're chasing along after whatever it is that you can't quite catch, and every gay person you encounter is sleazy, crooked, second rate, and generally unpleasant.''

''Or so it has seemed,'' I said.

''And, being a basically decent guy, despite the smart mouth, you fear that maybe you are prejudiced and it's clouding your judgment.''

''Also true, except for the smart mouth part.''

''Same thing happens to me with blacks,'' Farrell said. ''I spend two months on a drug-related homicide and everybody's black, and everybody's a vicious sleazebag, and I begin to wonder, is it me?''

''Neither one of us gets to deal with the best parts of a culture,'' I said.

''No. We deal with the worst. You got a case involving murder and blackmail, most of the people you meet are going to be scumbags.''

''Regardless of race, creed, or color,'' I said. ''Or sexual orientation.''

''And not because of race, creed, color, or sexual orientation,'' Farrell said.

''You mean homos aren't any better than the rest of us?'' I said.

''Most of us are,'' Farrell said, ''but not all of us.''

''How disappointing.''

''I know,'' Farrell said.

There was a big picture window in the front of the bar. The sun was west of us now and throwing long shadows onto the street outside. Men in suits carrying briefcases sidled in for a few fast ones before they got the train to Dover. It wasn't a place where women came much.

''Shall we have another beer?'' I said.

Farrell grinned at me.

''We'd be fools not to,'' he said.

CHAPTER THIRTY

I spent the rest of the afternoon in my office with a pad of lined yellow paper drawing little connection diagrams among the principals in the Prentice Lamont case. None of them seemed very useful, but that just made the exercise like all the other ones I had been through. Maybe it was time to get the cops into it. I knew Quirk when he tried the window Lamont had jumped from would agree with me that the suicide smelled bad. But with the cops came the press, and Robinson Nevins would be frequently mentioned in connection with the murder of a gay man. This was not, I was pretty sure, what he'd wanted when Hawk brought him to me.

Twice the phone rang, and both times, when I answered there was nothing but the sound of someone not talking at the other end. I did business with enough wackos that it could be one of several, but at the moment my money was on KC Roth. After the second one I dialed *69 and the phone rang for a while but no one answered, which meant nothing. KC could have shut off her answering machine. She could be refusing to answer. She could have called from a phone booth which was now ringing to the empty sidewalk. Or it could have been someone else doing these things.

It was after six when I left the office and walked down Berkeley Street toward my apartment. When I turned right onto Marlborough Street I saw her hiding behind a tree across from my apartment. When I got to my apartment entry I turned and looked over at the tree.

"KC," I said. "You're slightly larger than the tree trunk. I can see you."

She came out from behind the tree and walked toward me. She was dressed in black. She wore a large black hat, and her face, pale in contrast to her outfit, was tragic.

"I can't stay away from you," she said.

"Work on it," I said.

"I think of you all the time."

"How about the stalker," I said. "He come back?"

"No. I need to talk with you."

"Go ahead."

"Can we go upstairs?"

"No."

"Afraid?"

"Yes."

She looked up at me with her head lowered. She looked like an old Hedy Lamarr publicity still.

"Of me or yourself?" she said.

"You," I said.

"Damn you, can't you understand how desperate I am. I've been abandoned, betrayed, my husband has left me, I'm being stalked."

"I don't think you're being stalked anymore," I said.

"You caught him?"

"Yep."

"And?"

"I reasoned with him."

"Who?"

"Louis Vincent," I said.

"Louis?"

"Sorry."

"Louis—oh my god," she said and fell forward into my arms.

I held onto her and waited while she cried a little. When she stopped crying I let her go. She stayed where she was, leaning hard against me.

"Stand straight," I said.

"I can't," she said. "It's too much, too awful."

I gave her a couple of seconds and when she didn't stop leaning in to me, I stepped suddenly back away from her. She lurched forward and caught herself, and got her balance.

When she was on her own balance again her face darkened and she looked at me.

"You unutterable bastard," she said, and turned and strode away.

Her hips swung angrily as she headed toward Arlington Street. Unutterable, I thought. Not bad.

CHAPTER THIRTY-ONE

Hawk and I were drinking draught beer in a joint across from the Fleet Center. The Fleet Center had replaced the old Garden, and I could tell that the joint was trying to go along with the upscale clientele, because there was a bowl of cashews on the bar. I had several. So did Hawk.

"Usually it's a fight to see who gets the six cashews in a bowl of mixed nuts," I said.

"Kind of ruins the competition," Hawk said. "When they all cashews."

We drank some beer.

"You got that stalker thing worked out?" Hawk said.

"Yes, I identified the stalker and explained to him why he should stop it."

"Firmly," Hawk said.

"Quite."

"Good," Hawk said. "Don't like stalkers."

"Only problem is now getting rid of the stalkee."

Hawk turned his head slowly and looked at me and his eyes were bright with pleasure.

"She taken a liking to you?"

"You might say."

"Hear victims do that sometimes."

"Sometimes," I said.

"You say she good-looking?"

"Un huh."

"And, you ain't available, being as how you in love and all."

"True."

"Maybe you can divert her my way," Hawk said. "She'll thank you for it."

"I'll keep that option in mind."

We emptied the bowl of cashews, and the bartender came over and refilled it and drew us two more beers. Way upscale.

"How we doing with Robinson?"

"We?"

"Yeah, you and me. We finding out anything?"

"We figure Prentice was killed," I said.

"'Cause of how he couldn't have opened the window," Hawk said.

I nodded.

"And we're pretty sure he was blackmailing people," I said.

"How about at the university?"

"I know that the rumor of his relationship to Prentice was introduced by Lillian Temple and a guy named Bass Maitland."

"Lillian from Cambridge," Hawk said.

"Clearly. And Bass is her boyfriend."

"Lillian got a boyfriend?"

"Maybe when she lets her hair down and takes off her glasses," I said.

"They don't do that in Cambridge," Hawk said.

I shrugged. "We know that both Lillian and Bass are friends with Amir Abdullah," I said.

"Which tell you something about them," Hawk said.

There were still cashews left. I took a couple.

"And we know that Amir had met Prentice because Prentice wrote about him in his little magazine."

"So there a connection from Prentice through Amir to Lillian Cambridge and her boyfriend."

"Bass Maitland. Yeah there is."

We both drank some beer. The bar was nearly empty in the middle of the afternoon. The television above the bar was dark. There was no music playing on the jukebox. The light from the street filtered quietly in through the front windows.

"You know what I thinking?" Hawk said.

"Maybe," I said.

"I thinking that if the kid Prentice banking a quarter of million out of the blackmail gig then it too good a gig to end when he die.''

"And you're thinking it might be a good idea to keep an eye on the ones doing the magazine now."

"Yowzah."

"That would be Walt and Willie."

"You know them?"

"Yes."

"They business partners or are they a couple?"

"Couple, I think."

"So one's in it they probably both in it."

"Maybe," I said.

"They know you too?"

"Yeah."

"So we'll go by tomorrow," Hawk said, "and you point them out to me and I'll watch them for a while."

"Christ," I said, "almost sounds like a plan."

"Do," Hawk said, "don't it."

CHAPTER
THIRTY-TWO

Pearl the wonder dog was staying with me while Susan was at a two-day conference in Atlanta. We were lying in my bed watching the Braves game on cable when the phone rang.

A woman's voice said, "Is Susan there?"

"No," I said, "she's not. Can I take a message?"

"Does she make a lot of noise when you fuck her?" the voice said.

"Mostly she yells 'bravo,' " I said.

"I'll bet she lays there like an old laundry bag," the voice said.

"KC," I said. "Stop being a pain in the ass."

"There's a letter for you," she said, "in your mailbox downstairs."

Then she hung up. I thought about not looking, but that would be childish, so I got up, put on my pants, stuck a gun in my back pocket, and went down to look in my mailbox. The letter was there. Hand delivered obviously, no stamp, and no address, only my name. I took it and went back upstairs. Pearl was still on the bed though she had raised her head and was looking annoyed. I got back into bed beside her and opened the letter. It was handwritten in blue ink by someone who had been taught that a person was judged on her penmanship.

I think about you and Susan all the time. Is it still romantic or does she just undress and lay on the bed? Do you take off her clothes for her, slowly, one garment at a

time until she's naked? Are you naked when you do it? Or
do you undress after she's undressed? Does she respond?
Is she lively? Does she know a lot of tricks? Is she kinky?
Or is she just the kind of prude who closes her eyes and
lets you do what you want to her? She is so smart and
sarcastic I have often wondered if she could ever be genuine
enough to enjoy sex the way I do. The way we would, you
and I. I would give you everything. Does Susan? I would
ask nothing in return. Does Susan? You could still be with
Susan. And have me on the side. And when you were with
me, you might learn things that Susan can't teach you.

The letter made me uncomfortable. A little girl talking dirty
without using bad words. It always interested me that people had
a lot more trouble writing a dirty word than they did saying it.
It was also very uncomfortable to be the object of salacious
fantasy. The idea that a good-looking woman would think such
things about me was attractive. The reality was embarrassing. It
also made me think about why KC had trouble with men. She
thought that it was about sex, when what it was about was love.
It made me sorry for her. I could try to explain but she wouldn't
understand it, and, worse, if she did understand it she wouldn't
believe it.

"KC is doomed," I said to Pearl.

Pearl opened her eyes and looked at me without raising her
head. I didn't follow up the remark so she lost interest and closed
her eyes again. On television Andres Galarraga hit a hanging
curveball into the general area of Buckhead scoring Chipper
Jones ahead of him, and the ball game was over. I clicked off
the television and lay quietly beside Pearl thinking about KC. I
wondered if in fact I would learn something by sleeping with
her.

"You never know," I said to Pearl.

Pearl had discerned already that I was not looking for an answer so she moved her ear slightly to let me know she was
listening, but she didn't open her eyes. I was hungry. I got up
and went to the kitchen and made one and a half ham sandwiches
on light rye with dark mustard. I brought it back into the bedroom with a bottle of Sam Adams White Ale, got back into bed,

gave Pearl her half, and ate my sandwich, and drank my beer from the bottle.

"We're going to have to do something about KC," I said.

Pearl was engaged with her half sandwich.

"If only I knew what."

Pearl had mustard on her muzzle, she wiped it on the spread as I spoke. I drank some beer and had another bite of sandwich.

"This may be," I said to Pearl, "a job for Susan."

Pearl stood up, turned around three times, and settled back down with a large sigh. Clearly it was enough chitchat for the night.

THIRTY-THREE

It was time to pay some more attention to Lillian Temple. I called the Brandeis alumni office and got her current address from them. Alumni offices know your address when even the IRS can't find you. I called the university English department to make sure she wasn't teaching any night classes. Which she wasn't. The secretary sounded a bit offended that I would think she might be.

At about six o'clock in the evening I got in my car and drove over to Cambridge. Susan wasn't due back until the next morning, so I took Pearl with me. We parked outside Lillian's apartment building on Kirkland Street and waited. I didn't know what I was waiting for, but I often didn't. I was trying to figure out a way to get information from a hostile witness.

Pearl and I watched the sights and sounds of Cambridge pass by the car. Pearl reacted only to other dogs, and then with hostility, otherwise she rested her head placidly on the backseat and stared.

"Cambridge was placed here," I said, "across the river from Boston to provide comic relief."

A woman came by with an ugly black dog wearing a bandanna. Pearl barked at her. Or maybe it was her owner. Across the street Lillian Temple came out of the door to her building and walked across the street behind the car. It was a cool night. I cracked the windows.

"I gotta go," I said to Pearl, "you gotta stay. I'll be back."

I locked the car doors and followed Lillian down Kirkland

Street toward Mass Ave. It was still light, but she seemed a single-minded person, like many in Cambridge, who didn't pay much attention to what was happening around her. She took no notice of me tagging along behind. At Mass Ave she turned left and walked toward Harvard Square. There were some guys in native garb playing Peruvian pipes outside the Harvard Coop. Three or four people asked me for money. One offered to sell me a newspaper called *Spare Change,* "the newspaper by and for the homeless." There was a guy beating rhythm on the bottom of a series of different-sized inverted buckets. There were many kids with ring-pierced body parts and pastel hair hanging around the subway kiosk. Harvard students, and future Harvard students, parents, faculty, and staff all moved about the square among the street people ignoring the traffic and the traffic laws. There was a diverse variety of cops around the square. MBTA cops hanging at the subway entrance, Cambridge cops lingering near the corner of JFK and Brattle, a motorcycle cop with gleaming boots parked near Cardullo's, Harvard cops standing outside the Holyoke Center near the perpetual chess games.

Lillian turned right at Nini's corner and went down Brattle Street to The Casablanca bar and restaurant. When I got inside she was at the bar. It was about 7:20 on Thursday night and the bar was half empty. Or half full depending on how much you'd been drinking. I slid onto a bar stool beside her. She paid no attention to me. But she was aware of at least a male shape beside her because she looked at her watch sort of obviously to let me know she was waiting for someone and was not available. She ordered a glass of white wine, making it a longer process than it might have been by asking what kinds they had and how much it cost. She settled on a modest California chardonnay. I ordered a draught beer. I looked around on the bar, no cashews. They didn't seem to care about becoming upscale. Maybe they already were upscale. Lillian sipped her wine and looked ostentatiously at her watch again, lest one of the unaccompanied males, made reckless by animal lust, proposition her. She made no eye contact with anyone. Everything in her being vibrated with *I'm-waiting-for-someone.*

"Excuse me," I said. "Do you come here often?"

She fixed me with a withering stare, which changed slowly into recognition, which changed slowly into anxiety.

"Oh," she said, "it's you."

"Yes it is," I said.

"I'm waiting for someone," she said, and drank some of her wine.

"Really?"

"Yes. Bass, Bass Maitland."

She said the name as if it would make me slide off the stool and scuttle for the door. I held fast. She drank some more wine.

"While you're waiting," I said, "may I buy you a glass of wine?"

"I . . . I'd . . . I would rather you didn't," she said.

"Okay," I said.

I sat and looked at her. She looked at me and looked at her watch and glanced around the bar casually, the way a rat does when it's cornered. I drank a little beer. She finished her wine. I was quiet, still looking at her with a friendly look. Spenser— large but pleasant. She looked at her empty wineglass. She glanced at me and smiled a half smile. And glanced quickly down the bar toward the door to remind me that Bass was imminent. I remained calm.

"Offer still stands," I said.

"Oh, well, very well. It's kind of you."

I gestured to the bartender.

"Martin," I said, "a glass of white wine, for the lady."

"You've been here before," she said.

"I've been everywhere before," I said in perfect imitation of Humphrey Bogart.

She didn't seem to recognize it.

"Really?" she said.

Martin brought the wine and looked at my beer. I shook my head.

"Sure, the other guy is Gary," I said. "Impressive, isn't it."

She smiled politely. Badinage didn't seem her strongest suit. She drank nearly half of her new glass of wine. Maybe that was her strongest suit. I didn't say anything. She looked around the bar again. I had a swallow of beer. She drank most of the rest of her wine. I nodded at Martin. She checked the doorway, looked at her watch, finished her wine, and Martin brought her another one.

"Oh, I really couldn't," she said.

"Okay," I said.

She looked at the fresh glass of wine. A trickle of moisture ran down the side of the cold glass.

"I don't mean to be ungracious," she said.

"No offense," I said.

She looked at the wine. I swallowed a little more beer. She picked up the wine and drank some.

"No point in being stubborn," she said and smiled at me thinly.

She was wearing black sandals and a loose ankle-length black dress with pink and yellow flowers printed on it. Her hair was pulled back tight to her head and culminated in a long braid. Her skin was pale, and she had on no makeup except some pink lipstick.

"How are you doing in your, ah, investigation," she said.

"Depends on how you define progress," I said. "I'm no closer to finding out whether Robinson Nevins got jobbed in his tenure bid, but I have found out that Prentice Lamont was a blackmailer, and that he was murdered."

"Murdered?"

"Un huh."

"How do you know that?"

"I detected it."

"And what's this about blackmail?" Lillian said.

She was nearly finished with her third glass of wine and when Gary went by she gestured him for a refill.

"He was blackmailing homosexuals who would rather not be outed," I said.

She finished her previous glass and handed it to Gary as he set the new glass down.

"My God," she said.

"Exactly," I said.

She looked at me uneasily for a moment.

"Did you come here to talk to me?" she said.

"I followed you here," I said.

"Followed?"

"Yep. I need to know who told you that Lamont's suicide was connected to Robinson Nevins."

"I have already told you that is confidential information."

"Not anymore," I said. "I haven't gone to the cops yet, because I'm trying to save everybody a lot of grief. But if I can't solve this myself, I will take it to the cops, and you can tell the homicide guys, who, by the way, are nowhere near as charming as I am.''

''Homicide?''

''You are going to have to tell, Professor Temple. You can tell me, now, or you can tell the cops soon.''

She looked at the door again, and around the bar, and at her watch, and drank some wine and turned to me and said, ''Difficult choices.''

''Not really,'' I said. ''One's easy, one's hard, same outcome.''

She stared at me for a moment, looked away, looked down at her wine, looked back at me, but couldn't hold the look.

Staring at the wineglass she said, ''Will he have to know I told?''

''Probably not,'' I said. ''I can't guarantee it, but I won't tell if I don't have to.''

She nodded, still staring into the wineglass.

''Amir,'' she said.

''Amir Abdullah?''

''Yes.''

''He told you Prentice Lamont and Robinson Nevins were having an affair?''

''Yes. And that Robinson broke it off cruelly and Prentice killed himself.''

''He say how he knew this?''

''No.''

''And you took it and reported it whole, as he told it.''

''I had no—have no—reason to doubt him. Amir is a very principled man.''

I had some reservations about exactly how principled Amir Abdullah was, but I let them slide, because Bass Maitland had arrived. He was strolling in from the front door. By the way Lillian was looking at him he might have been walking on water.

''Bass,'' she said.

''Hi, Lil,'' he said in his big round satisfied voice.

He was wearing a seersucker jacket, well-faded blue jeans, a black polo shirt with the collar turned up, and deck shoes, no socks.

Lillian said, "You remember Mr. . . . the detective we talked to."

"Spenser," I said.

"Oh, absolutely. How are you?"

He gave me the kind of big firm handshake that a big firm man would give. He was so pleased with himself that it was infectious. I almost liked him.

"Is this a coincidence," he said with a big smile, "or are you staking us out?"

"Holding your place for you," I said, and stood up.

"Appreciate it."

He took my seat and smiled again, like an affable crocodile. He was probably a very principled man, too. So were they all, all principled men. And women. There were few things more annoying than a visibly principled person. Or more troublesome. Most of the ones I'd met could have used a little uncertainty to dilute their principled-ness. But it didn't seem a fruitful topic to discuss with Bass and Lillian, so I said good-bye and went off to get my dog.

CHAPTER
THIRTY-FOUR

The call came from KC Roth just after I had settled in to watch
the Sox and the Angels from the West Coast.

"Come quickly," she said. "Please. I need you."

She sounded teary.

"What's your problem?"

"Louis."

"What about Louis?"

"He came back."

"Really?"

"Oh, please, come quickly. Please."

"Why?"

"He, he . . . please come."

"What did he do?"

"He . . . violated me."

"Do you mean he raped you?"

She was silent.

"Did he rape you?" I said.

"Yes."

"Have you called the police?"

"Oh, God no, I can't talk about this with the police. I, please,
I have to see you, you're the only one."

"When did this happen," I said.

"Just now. He just left."

"He's gone."

"Yes. He beat me and he violated me."

"Have you been to the doctor?"

"No. I told you. I can't . . ."

"Don't take a shower," I said. "Don't bathe or wash yourself. Stay still. I'll be there in half an hour. Will you be all right until then?"

"Yes."

"Okay. When I get there I'm going to take you to the doctor."

"No."

"Unless you agree to that I won't come."

"I . . . I can't . . ." She was crying.

"You'll have to promise. Otherwise I'll hang up and call the Reading cops and it'll be you and them."

"No . . . oh why are you so awful?"

"Promise?"

She was silent, sobbing. I waited.

"Oh yes, goddamn you," she said and hung up.

I got dressed and drove up to Reading. She was hugging herself looking out the door waiting for me. Until I saw her I thought she might be making it up. Now I was pretty sure she wasn't. Someone had slapped her around pretty good. Her upper lip was swollen and one eye was puffed. It would be shut by morning. She had on a white tee shirt and gray sweatpants and moccasins. Her hair was a mess.

"Oh God," she said, and backed away as I came in.

"Come on," I said. "Hospital."

"You're really going to make me?"

"You bet," I said.

I took her arm. She flinched away for a moment. But I kept hold and she relaxed enough to go with me.

The on-call gyno who showed up at the emergency room was a young woman with red hair and a good backside who whisked into the examining room, took one look at KC, and whisked me out with one brisk all-inclusive gesture. I sat in the waiting area and looked at people with bruises and cuts and breathing problems and stomach pains as they came and went. I read several ancient copies of *People* magazine, which left me feeling like I'd eaten too much fudge.

After about an hour, the gyno came out and said, "Mr. Spenser?"

"Me," I said.

"Come in please."

I went in. KC was in a johnny and those silly slippers that they give you. Her hair had been combed and her face washed and she seemed a little foggy. A large black woman in a nurse suit hovered around and looked at me disapprovingly.

"I'm Dr. Tripp," the red-haired woman said. "Mrs. Roth says I may speak freely with you. What is your relationship to her?"

"Employee," I said.

"In what capacity?"

"I'm a detective. She hired me to prevent this from happening to her."

"She may wish to rethink that," Dr. Tripp said.

"She may," I said. "Was she raped?"

"She was."

"No doubt of it?"

"None. There's vaginal bruising. There's semen. The police have been notified."

KC stared at her.

"No," she said thickly. "I don' wan' that."

"Mrs. Roth, I'm required to," she said. "Neither you nor I have a choice."

"Tranquilizer?" I said.

"Valium. You're not with the police."

"No. I'm a private detective."

"Really," she said. "Do you know who did this?"

"I think so," I said.

"No. He din't," KC said. "I will swear he din't."

Dr. Tripp stared at her.

"You'll protect the man who did this?"

"I don' know who did," KC said.

Dr. Tripp looked at me. I shrugged.

"I would like to keep her overnight," Dr. Tripp said.

"I think that's a good idea," I said. "Maybe you can put the cops off until tomorrow."

"One reason I want her to stay," Dr. Tripp said.

"Will you stay wi' me?" she said to me. "I won' stay 'less you stay wi' me."

"It's permitted," Dr. Tripp said.

"Oh good," I said.

Spending the night sitting in a chair by KC Roth's bedside was about as appealing as a Howard Stern film festival. I took in a lot of air through my nose and let it out the same way. Dr. Tripp and the black nurse and KC all stared at me with various degrees of male-oriented hostility.

"Sure," I said. "Be glad to."

CHAPTER THIRTY-FIVE

In the morning, under the stern gaze of Dr. Tripp, the Reading cops were solicitous, and KC was uninformative, and I was tired. KC insisted that she didn't know her assailant. The cops clearly did not believe her but couldn't figure out why she'd protect him, and neither could I. They had a young female assistant from the Middlesex DA's office who seemed bright and sympathetic and was pretty clever in some of her questions but not bright enough, or apparently sympathetic enough. KC refused to change her story and finally resorted to crying, which worked. The crying may have been sincere. She had been beaten and raped, but I also knew that she could cry at will, and life had made me cynical.

After the cops left and the bright young sympathetic DA went with them, Dr. Tripp told KC that a social worker would stop by to talk with her in a while. And that Dr. Tripp felt that KC should stay another night. KC nodded. Her crying had dwindled to sniffling. She patted her unswollen eye with a Kleenex and blew her nose and sat up a little higher in the bed.

"Keep that eye cold," Dr. Tripp said as she went out.

We were alone. I handed KC one of the compresses from the tray on her bedside table. She held it against her nearly closed eye.

"No one here but you and me," I said. "I won't tell, you have my word on it, but I have to be sure. You said it was Vincent."

She started to cry again. Not boo hoo, more sniff sniff, but still crying. She seemed to be hiding behind the cold compress.

"Dip that in the ice water," I said. "It was, wasn't it?"

She cried some more.

"Damn it, KC, yes or no? You don't have to speak. Just nod. You said it was Vincent."

Nod.

"Thank you," I said.

We were quiet. She sniffled a little more and stopped.

"Will you kill him for me?" she said.

"No," I said. "But I'll make sure he leaves you alone."

"You promise?"

"I promise."

"I think he's a little crazy," she said. "You know how it's crazy time when a romance breaks up."

"Um hmm."

"I can count on you, can't I?"

"Yes."

"I feel as if I've known you all my life."

"You haven't," I said, "and you're a little crazy yourself, right now. But you'll be better."

"Of course I'm crazy," she said. "What I've gone through. I have a right to be crazy."

"Of course you do," I said. "But only for a while."

The social worker stuck her head around the partly open door.

"Can I come in?" she said.

"Tell her yes," KC said to me.

"Come in," I said.

The social worker was a thin-faced black-haired woman wearing round glasses with green rims.

"I'm Amy Coulter," she said, "from Social Services. Dr. Tripp asked me to come and see you."

"Sit down," I said. "I'm leaving anyway."

"Where are you going?" KC said.

"Home," I said. "Sleep."

"You'll come back?"

"Like esophageal reflux," I said.

I always tried to make my similes appropriate to the ambiance. Surprisingly neither Amy Coulter nor KC remarked on it. Too bad Dr. Tripp wasn't there. She'd appreciate my kind of quality medical humor.

CHAPTER THIRTY-SIX

I stopped for coffee and a couple of donuts, and then went straight to Susan's house and let myself into her living space. I submitted to five minutes or so of lapping and jumping about from Pearl before I got her quieted down enough so I could take off my clothes and lie on the bed in my shorts. Always game for a nap, Pearl jumped up on the bed, turned around several times, and got ready to lie down beside me. I was asleep before she did.

When I woke up Pearl was gone. I looked at my watch. It was 6:20 in the evening. I got up and walked around the house. I noticed that Susan's purse was on the front hall table, and Pearl's leash was gone. I went back into the bedroom and took a long shower and shaved in the shower and put on clean clothes from the wardrobe stash I kept at Susan's place, and was pouring two ounces of Dewar's over a lot of ice in a tall glass when Pearl and Susan came back from their walk. Pearl bounded about the way she does when she knows supper is imminent, and Susan, more restrained, came over and gave me a kiss on the mouth.

"Good to see you up and about," Susan said. "When I came up from the office and found you I thought you might be dead."

I poured club soda over the ice in my tall glass, getting it as close to the top as I could, without it being so full I couldn't pick it up without spilling.

"Did you have a plan for how to deal with that?" I said.

"If you were still dead when I came back from walking the baby," Susan said, "I was going to call someone."

I got a bag of Kibbles 'N Bits dog food out of the cupboard and put a cup and a half's worth into Pearl's bowl. I knew it was Pearl's bowl because it said Pearl in violet script on the outside.

Susan said, "She likes it with cheese, remember."

I got some shredded cheese out of the refrigerator and sprinkled some over the food and put it down on the floor. Pearl did like it with cheese. She also liked it without cheese, or with sawdust. Susan went into her bedroom, and I sat at the counter and sipped my scotch and soda. Susan came out in a while barefooted, in a dark blue tank top and white shorts, with her hair combed, and wearing fresh lip gloss.

"Got any snacks?" I said. "I appear to have slept through lunch."

Susan got an elegant wine goblet sort of the color of sea mist from another cabinet and poured some Merlot into it, and took a small sip.

"I have some rice cakes," Susan said. "And some broccoli sprouts, and . . ." She got up and opened her refrigerator door and gazed in. ". . . half a bagel."

"Gee, a cornucopia," I said.

Susan had great glassware and wonderful china and beautiful silverware and no food.

"And some shredded cheese, but that's for the baby . . ." She closed the refrigerator and opened the cupboard. ". . . and some bite-sized shredded wheat."

She turned and looked at me optimistically, as if I might like shredded wheat and broccoli sprouts with my scotch and soda.

"That's okay," I said. "We can order out."

"Chinese?" Susan said.

"Yes, a bunch of everything, and tell them to hurry. In a little while it will be a medical emergency."

Susan called and ordered a bunch of everything including some broccoli, sauce on the side, and steamed rice. Then she came back and sat across the counter from me and took a sip of her wine.

"What I don't get," I said, "is this creep beats her up and rapes her and she won't tell the cops."

"But she admitted it to you."

"Yes."

"Well, that aside, consider it from her perspective," Susan said.

She was leaning her elbows on the counter holding her sea mist wine goblet in both hands, looking at me over the top of it. I had a fresh drink.

"Okay," I said, "she leaves her husband for the man of her dreams and the man of her dreams turns out to be an abusive rapist."

"Bad mistake," Susan said. "But to report him to the police is to certify that mistake."

"So?"

"So maybe it means her husband wins and she loses," Susan said.

"And she'd rather shield her rapist than lose to her husband?"

"It's not just that she loses, it's that he has the triumphant gratification of seeing her be humiliated for her own folly. It might be worse for her than rape."

"So why does she tell me?"

"Because she has to tell someone. Because she needs you to protect her. Because she somehow has learned already that you won't judge her. Because you may have replaced, what's his name?"

"Louis Vincent."

"You may have replaced Louis Vincent as the man of her new dreams."

"Well," I said. "You would certainly know what that's like."

Susan paid no attention. When she was thinking she was filled completely by the subject of her thoughts.

"And," Susan said and smiled slightly, "because you knew anyway. And she'd cozy up to you by making you the only one she'd tell."

The doorbell rang. Pearl went ballistic as she always does when the doorbell rings. I went downstairs and paid for the Chinese food and brought it back up. The smell of fresh delivered Chinese food almost defines anticipation. Pearl barked once at me when I came into the living room before she realized I wasn't a bell-ringing intruder, then got a whiff of the food and became very focused. I put it on the counter prepared to eat it from the cartons, but of course Susan had set the counter and put out place mats and silverware and a pair of ivory chopsticks for herself. She liked to eat with chopsticks. I did not. Susan served.

"If she won't tell the cops, of course, this becomes my problem."

"Oh really," Susan said.

"What do you mean 'oh really'?"

"Given what we know about her, and the letter you showed me," Susan said, "isn't that exactly what she would want?"

I thought about it.

"Yes," I said. "But she couldn't have contrived the rape."

"No, I'm sure she didn't. But she has exploited it, consciously or not, to serve what she thinks is her best interest."

"Which is me."

"Yes."

"Because I'm so debonair?"

"Because KC is a cliché. For whatever reasons, she needs a knight to gallop in and save her, and if it's a debonair one, so much the better."

"My strength is as the strength of ten . . ."

"I know," Susan said. "What did you promise her."

"What makes you think I promised her anything?"

"Because I have been with you for a very long time, Sir Percival. What did you promise her."

"That I'd make sure he left her alone."

"Perfect," Susan said. "What are you going to do?"

"I spoke with him once," I said.

"And it didn't take," Susan said. "How vigorous are you prepared to be?"

"I gave my word," I said.

"Perhaps Hawk," Susan said.

"No. Hawk didn't give his word. I gave mine. I can't ask him to do something because I don't want to do it."

"No," Susan said, "I know you can't."

We were silent. Pearl put both front paws on the edge of the counter and gazed at the food. I gave her an egg roll and she dropped down and dashed to the couch to eat it.

"Vincent must be in the grip of his own pathologies," Susan said. "You are able to frighten most people off."

"I know."

"You won't kill him," Susan said.

It wasn't a question.

"No."

"Perhaps you and Hawk could broach the subject to him together."

I nodded.

"Many white men are more afraid of black men than they are of other whites," I said. "If he's one of them we could exploit his racism."

"My thought exactly," Susan said.

"Can you do anything to help KC?"

"You mean professionally?"

"Whatever. She sure as hell needs something."

"I can't be her shrink," Susan said. "I've known her too long, and I am not, ah, above the fray."

"You're not?"

"You may recall a few phrases from the lovely little mash note she stuck in your mailbox: Such as: 'when you were with me, you might learn things that Susan can't teach you.' "

"That means nothing to me," I said.

"It means something to me," Susan said.

"Are we feeling a little unprofessional jealousy?" I said.

"We are feeling a little unprofessional desire to kick her fat little ass," Susan said.

I was drinking scotch and soda and eating chicken with cashews and the girl of my dreams was jealous. I smiled happily.

CHAPTER

THIRTY-SEVEN

Hawk came into my office at about 9:30 carrying a brown paper bag. With him was a barrel-bodied black man with short, slightly bowed legs and long arms. The black man had gray hair and the kind of amused eyes that Robert Benchley used to have. Hawk put the bag on my desk and pulled one of my office chairs around, and the gray-haired black man sat in it.

"Spenser," Hawk said. "Bobby Nevins."

I stood and came around and shook hands with Nevins. Hawk went to the Mister Coffee machine on top of my file cabinet and began to make some coffee. I looked in the paper bag. There was a large square loaf-shaped something wrapped in aluminum foil.

"Corn bread," Bobby Nevins said. "Hawk always like corn bread."

Bobby Nevins was a legend. He'd trained fighters for more than fifty years. All of his fighters could fight. All of them were in shape. None left the ring broke. None were strolling queer street. In a business riddled with charlatans his word was good. Hawk had the coffee brewing and came back and sat down in the other client chair.

"Bobby in town to see about how we doing with his kid," Hawk said.

I nodded, thinking about the corn bread.

"And I got some things you don't know 'bout yet."

"Would everybody like me to open the corn bread up while the coffee's brewing?" I said.

"Sure," Hawk said. "Okay with you, Bobby?"

"'Course," Nevins said.

His voice came from deep in his chest and seemed to resonate in his barrel body before it emerged. I unwrapped the corn bread and set it on the unfolded foil in the middle of my desk. It smelled good. From my desk drawer I got a large switchblade knife, which I had once taken away from an aggressive but clumsy drug dealer, and now used as a letter opener. With it I cut three squares of corn bread. Hawk brought over the coffee. I took some corn bread. And chewed it carefully and swallowed it and drank some coffee.

"My compliments to the chef," I said.

"Always liked to cook a little," Nevins said. "Now I gotten older got more time. Hawk says this thing about my boy is turning into a hair ball."

"Hawk's right," I said. "Thing is I still don't know quite why he was jobbed on the tenure thing. It seems like the only thing I can't find out. Meanwhile I've got a murder and some blackmailing—which, as far as I know, has nothing to do with your kid."

"Anybody paying you for this?"

"Corn bread will do," I said.

"Ain't right, you not getting paid."

"I owe Hawk a favor."

Hawk snorted.

"*A* favor?"

"A favor or two," I said.

Nevins nodded. He ate some more corn bread and drank some more coffee. Hawk got up and took Nevins' cup and refilled it, pouring in a little milk from the mini-refrigerator, stirring in two spoonfuls of sugar. He brought the cup back and set it in front of Nevins on the corner of my desk. Nevins picked it up and took a sip and held the cup.

"Thank you, Hawk," he said.

Hawk nodded. Nevins looked at me.

"You think Robinson is queer?"

"Don't know," I said.

"I don't either. Hard thing for a boy to tell his father, I imagine."

I nodded.

"He's forty years old," Nevins said, "ain't never been married."

"Hawk and I have never been married either," I said.

"How you know about me?" Hawk said.

"Who would marry you?"

"Okay," Hawk said. "You got a point."

Nevins paid no attention.

"Thing is it don't matter much," he said. "Still my son."

"Yes," I said.

"I was forty-two when he was born," Nevins said. "Coulda been his grandfather. His mother was only twenty-three, schoolteacher, fresh out of college. I coulda been her daddy."

Hawk and I were silent, drinking coffee, listening to Nevins. There was no age in Nevins' voice, no weakness in him.

"She left when she was thirty."

"Another man?" I said.

"Another one and another one," Nevins said. "Probably still going on."

There was no resentment in Nevins' voice either, nor remorse, nor anger, nor self-pity, only the sound of retrospection.

"Always sent her money for Robinson, and, I say this for her, she never kept me from seeing him on the weekend. But I know she didn't like boxing, and I pretty sure she didn't like me, and I don't believe she kept quiet 'bout it to Robinson. So be hard for Robinson to feel real close to me. He was a real smart little kid. He loved to read. He was kind of scared of the fighters. I used to take him to the museum and the public library and places, never read much myself, but I knew that was where his life was going to go. Too bad I didn't know more about things like that. We could never talk much. Spent a lot of money getting him through Harvard College and all those other schools he went to so he could be a professor, and I think he knows that. Probably could tell his mother he was queer, but I don't think he could tell me."

"You want us to find that out?" Hawk said.

Nevins thought about this for a while, sipping his coffee slowly, looking past the cup at the long corridor of time past.

"No," he said. "Don't matter."

We were quiet.

"Tell me 'bout the murder and blackmail."

"I'll tell you what I know," I said, "and what I'm guessing."
Which I did.

Nevins didn't say a word as I talked. His gaze was steady and somehow both benign and stern. When I was through I looked at Hawk.

"You got something?" I said.

"Un huh."

"Were you planning to share it?"

"Un huh."

I cut another small piece of corn bread. I had learned from Susan that cutting off one small piece at a time was better for you even if you ate the whole thing one small piece at a time. Hawk got himself some more coffee. He looked at Nevins.

"Bobby?" he said.

Nevins shook his head. Hawk looked at me. I shook my head. Hawk came back and sat down.

"Been watching Walt and Willie," Hawk said.

He looked at Nevins.

"They the people inherited *OUTrageous* I told you about."

Nevins nodded. He was nearly motionless as he sat. Time made no difference to him.

"Might be they knew about the blackmail. Might be they carrying it on. So I'm watching them, see what develops."

"Sneak up on them in the dark better, too," I said.

"Like you could in a snowstorm," Hawk said. "Which one is the little blond queen?"

"Willie."

"He stepping out on Walt," Hawk said.

"Walt know this?"

"Don't know. Don't seem mad when he around Willie. Want to know who he stepping out with?"

"Yes I do."

"Your friend and mine, Amir Abdullah."

"Oh ho," I said.

"Oh ho?"

"Yes. That's what you say if you're a top-level sleuth and a clue falls out of a tree and hits you on the head."

Hawk looked at Nevins.

"Honkies are strange people, Bobby."

"What's the clue?" Nevins said.

"The connection between the *OUTrageous* folks and the tenure folks. Amir's the one who told the tenure committee that Robinson had an affair with Prentice Lamont. *OUTrageous* had a list of possible people to out with your son's name on it and the phrase 'research continues.' "

"So what does that mean?"

"Research continues?"

"No, what is the, ah, significance, of all that?"

"Hell, Mr. Nevins, I don't know. It's just more than we knew before. And maybe Abdullah got it from Willie, or maybe Willie got it from Abdullah—which would be my guess."

"Don't help my son get tenure."

"Not yet."

"Strange system," Nevins said. "Keep you for life or they fire you."

"I know."

"Robinson wants to be a professor at the university," Nevins said.

"We going to get that for him, Bobby," Hawk said.

I would have been happier if he hedged it a little, but Hawk wasn't much for hedging.

"I hope so," Nevins said.

Me too.

CHAPTER
THIRTY-EIGHT

I was taking a walk. Sometimes when I had to think I liked to walk along the river. Today was especially good for that because it was raining pleasantly. It was warm and there was no wind, just the steady moderate rain coming straight down and dimpling the dark surface of the river. I had on jeans and running shoes and a windbreaker and my old Boston Braves baseball hat. Impervious.

Before I got Robinson Nevins tenure at the university, I had the issue of Louis Vincent and KC Roth to resolve. I didn't have it in me to walk up and kill him. I'd killed people. And maybe I would again, but I'd always thought it was because I had to. Hawk would do it. He was more practical than I was. He didn't wait until he had to. He'd do it if it seemed a good solution to the problem—which it did. But I couldn't ask Hawk to do things I was too squeamish to do. What I needed to do was figure out what I was not too squeamish to do.

I crossed the little footbridge over Storrow Drive and onto the Esplanade and turned west and strolled upriver. The narrow strip of parkland ran along the Boston side of the Charles River all the way out to Watertown and beyond. In good weather it was crowded with people walking and jogging and walking dogs and bicycling and Rollerblading and sunbathing. Today, except for a few people who owned intrepid dogs, the space was pretty much mine. Not everyone understood about a walk in the rain. Pearl, for instance, despite her great hunting lineage, would not walk in the rain. Even for a cookie.

Squeamish was actually the wrong word for my hesitation. I would have, in fact, loved to throw Louis Vincent off a bridge. But it seemed somehow the wrong thing to do, and while I tried not to get hung up on abstractions more than I had to, I couldn't seem to get around this one. I could tell the cops he was the man, but as long as KC wouldn't testify, what could we do that was legal? Hitting him hadn't worked. I could hit him more, and harder. Which would be heartwarming, but if he was as obsessive as he seemed, it might merely wind him tighter. I needed KC to testify.

The racing crews in their eight-man shells were on the river, men's teams and women's teams, which meant, I supposed, that some of the shells were eight-woman shells, or that all of the shells were eight-person shells. The crew coaches, in motorboats, hovered near them like sheepdogs. During rest periods the rowers slumped over their oars as if they were dead, letting the rain beat down on them without regard.

I thought about Susan's analysis. KC's refusal to identify Louis Vincent seemed to be as much about her ex-husband as it was about Louis Vincent.

At the B.U. Bridge I turned back, my collar up, my Braves hat pulled down over my eyes, liking the feel of the rain as it came down in a straight easy fall, watching the idea coalesce. By the time I got back to my place the idea was nearly complete, or as complete as it could be.

I stripped off my wet clothes and tossed them in the washer, took a hot shower, toweled off, and put on fresh clothes. Then I went to the kitchen. It was 5:20 in the evening. Time enough for the first drink of the day, maybe past time. I filled a pint glass with ice, put in two ounces of scotch, and filled it with soda. I took the first sip. The first sip wasn't the best thing in the world, but it was in the top five. And trying to recapture the first sip is a reminder that maybe you really can't go home again. I picked up the glass and inspected my food supply. It was embarrassingly similar to Susan's. But there was a head of garlic and a can of black beans and some linguine and some biscuits left over from breakfast.

I put the biscuits in a low oven to warm. The coalescing idea unified and I knew what I was going to do. I drank a toast to my brain. Then I tucked a dish towel into my belt to make a little apron, the way my father used to, got out a knife and separated the garlic head into cloves and peeled the cloves. I cooked the garlic on low heat with some olive oil in a fry pan for a while, and while it was cooking I heated a large pot of water. When the water boiled I added a dash of olive oil and a little salt and put the linguine in. When the garlic cloves were soft I added some sherry, and as it began to cook down I opened the can of black beans and drained off the liquid and dumped them in with the sherry and olive oil and garlic and put a lid on the fry pan. I toasted my coalesced idea again and the glass was empty and I mixed another. It was still good, but it wasn't the first one. The first one wouldn't be available until tomorrow.

I sprinkled a little cilantro in among the black beans, garlic, olive oil, and sherry. When everything was cooked I tossed the black beans with the linguine and got out the biscuits and sat at my kitchen counter by myself and ate the pasta and sipped the scotch and soda and wondered if my plan would work. There was a lot I couldn't control, but it was a better plan than any of the others, except maybe just shooting Louis Vincent. But since I didn't think I should do that, and wouldn't ask Hawk to do it, and had promised KC that Louis Vincent would bother her no more, and since I had had two scotch and sodas, it seemed a very fine plan indeed, with every chance of succeeding. Of course, a lot depended on Burton Roth. But he'd seemed a solid guy when I'd met him, and I had hopes. On the other hand, if I didn't have hopes what the hell was I doing in this business. I could always make a fine living creating great suppers out of nothing.

CHAPTER THIRTY-NINE

Early spring had drifted into late spring and it was still raining the next morning. On my way to work, with my collar up and my hat pulled down, looking dashingly noir, I stopped into a store on Newbury Street called Bjoux, where I had been conspiring with the owner, a tall good-looking woman named Barbara Jordan, about a surprise birthday gift for Susan. Then I went to the office, and took time to clean up a few old business things still unresolved. I answered some mail, looked at my bank statements, and called a guy named Bill Poduska to ask him if he was going to charge me for helicopter services on a missing-child case I'd done last winter. I was hoping he might say it was pro bono, because the client hadn't paid me, even though I'd gotten the kid back. Bill apparently knew that, because he said there was no charge. I said thank you. Then I made some coffee, looked out at the rain for a while. It was an especially good rain because there was thunder and lightning with it and that always gave the weather a kind of charged tension that I enjoyed.

After watching the lightning and counting the seconds until I heard the thunder and figuring out by doing that how far away the storm was, and wondering if that actually was accurate, and then wondering why I in fact cared, I decided I had stalled on my plan long enough and called Burton Roth with somewhat less confidence than I had felt after two drinks the night before. We talked for half an hour and I had been right after all. He understood the problem and was prepared to help me solve it. Never a doubt in my mind. I told Roth I'd get back to him, and hung up just before Hawk came in with raindrops still beaded on his lavender silk trench coat.

"Got a plan?" Hawk said.

"Got a million," I said. "Or are you talking about a workable plan?"

Hawk unbuttoned his coat and went and stood looking out my office window at the rain falling on the corner of Berkeley and Boylston.

"Bobby worried about his kid," Hawk said.

"Even after he met me?" I said.

"Bobby don't know about you."

"I'm not so sure about me sometimes either."

"I gave him my word," Hawk said.

"Yeah. Thanks."

"So what you got in mind?"

"Well, I was thinking about pitching it in and becoming a caterer—you know? Leftovers R Us. Come in, take whatever there is in the house, fix up a tasty meal?"

Hawk continued to stare at the rain through my window. I went over and stood beside him and looked down. Puddles had formed and the raindrops hitting the puddles made tiny eruptions. The lightning skidded along the arch of the sky and shortly afterward the thunder cracked. It was dandy.

"I'd target the WASP market," I said.

Hawk nodded. The rain slithered in thick rivulets down the outside of my window. It diffused the lightning flash prismatically for a transitory moment.

"Be about a hundred million white guys in this country," Hawk said as the electricity crackled in the sky, "I end up with you."

"Talk about luck," I said.

"Talk about," Hawk said. "What we gonna do about Bobby's kid?"

"Do what we always do," I said. "Keep dragging on the end we got hold of, see what we pull out of the hole."

"What end we got hold of?"

"Willie and Amir."

"So we follow them and see what's at the other end."

"Exactly," I said.

"That your plan?"

"You bet," I said.

"And you do this for a living?"

"So far," I said.

"We gonna share?" Hawk said.

"Yes, you take Amir, I'll take Willie."

"Okay I give Amir a swat, I get the chance?"

"Long as he doesn't spot you tailing him," I said.

Hawk turned from the window.

"How you doing with that other gig, the stalker?"

"I'm working on it," I said.

"You doing as good with that as you are with this?" Hawk said.

"No."

Hawk nodded and smiled.

"Leftovers R Us," he said. "Might catch on."

On the street below, people were shielding themselves from the rain by various means, including but not limited to umbrellas. A woman went by holding her purse over her head, another used a briefcase. Several *Boston Globes* and at least one *Boston Herald* were also deployed.

"I figure I can buy a couple cases of cream of mushroom soup," I said. "And I'm in business."

"The basis of WASP cuisine," Hawk said. "While I walking around behind Amir Abdullah, you got any idea what I'm looking for?"

"We'll know it when we see it," I said. "We need to know two things—who threw Prentice Lamont out the window, and why Amir was trying to sink Robinson Nevins' tenure."

"'Cause Amir a creep?" Hawk said.

"Good enough for you and me, maybe not good enough for the university tenure committee."

"They overrule the English department," Hawk said.

"They can, Susan told me, and so can the dean," I said. "Though Susan says neither one likes to."

"So Robinson got a couple more shots."

"If we can come up with something," I said.

"We up against it I can always hold Amir upside down," Hawk said, "and shake him until something falls out."

"That's plan B," I said. "First we find out what we can by

watching. Otherwise while you're shaking him other people might scoot out of sight."

"What other people?"

"That's what we're watching to find out."

"Why you think there's other people?"

"Leads somewhere," I said. "Assume there aren't any other people, and we don't know what to do next."

"You caterers do be some deep philosophical motherfuckers," Hawk said.

"We do," I said.

CHAPTER FORTY

Before we could unleash ourselves on Amir and Willie we had Louis Vincent to attend to. It was a tricky one to time. I had shared my plan with Sgt. O'Connor of the Reading cops. He was keeping an eye on KC and reported that she was home. Burt Roth had given me his beeper number and said he'd be standing by. So it was all in place, at least for the moment, and if Louis Vincent came out to lunch this noontime we might be in business. If he didn't we'd have to innovate.

He did. I was standing in a doorway on the opposite corner of State and Congress so I could see him whichever door he came out. State Street was one way, so Hawk was idling his Jaguar, on the corner of State and Broad, two blocks down. Vincent walked out onto Congress Street wearing a Burberry trench coat and a tweed hat and turned the corner and headed down State Street toward the waterfront. I let him see me and as soon as he did he ran. It was a panic run. Hawk turned up onto State Street and was idling at the curb when I caught Vincent. Vincent tried to kick me and I turned my left hip and deflected the kick and nailed him on the chin with a right hook. He sagged, I caught him. Hawk was out of his car and had the back door open. I shoved Vincent in, and went in after him. Hawk was back in and behind the wheel by the time I got straightened up, and we were off to Reading. A couple of pedestrians stared after us.

Vincent took a while to get over the right hook, so he was quiet as we went down past North Station and through the old

West End. As Hawk went up onto the expressway at Leverett Circle, Vincent said, "What are you doing?"

"Shut up."

"You can't . . ."

I slapped him across the face. It was more startling than painful. He put his hands up in case I was going to do it again.

"Shut up."

Vincent was a quick study, one slap was enough. He didn't say another word as we went up Route 93. Hawk dialed Burt Roth's beeper, punched in his car phone number, and hung up. As we were passing Medford Square the car phone rang, Hawk spoke into it a moment, and hung up. Vincent looked worried but didn't say anything.

"He'll be there," Hawk said to me without turning his head.

Vincent looked more worried when we turned off at the Reading exit and even more worried when we headed north on Route 28 toward KC's place. A Reading police car was parked out front. Roth was in the parking lot in a green Subaru station wagon. When we pulled in, I got out and waved at the Reading cruiser. Sgt. O'Connor gave me a thumbs-up sign out the window as he pulled away. Hawk had gotten out and was standing by Vincent's door. I went around and opened it and jerked my head at Vincent.

"Where we going?" Vincent said.

Hawk reached in, got hold of his hair, and dragged him out headfirst.

"Hate a rapist," Hawk said.

Burt Roth got out of his car and walked toward us. And stopped in front of us and looked at Vincent. Roth's face had no expression.

"You know each other?" I said.

"Know of," Roth said. "We've never met."

"Who are you?" Vincent said.

"Burt Roth."

"Jesus."

"Let's go inside," I said.

"I don't want to go in," Vincent said.

I took his arm and moved him firmly toward the door. As I did so he had half an eye on Hawk.

"Nobody here cares anything at all about what you want, Louis."

I rang the doorbell and KC answered. Even here, in the face of what must have been a genuinely shocking event, her reaction had a theatricality about it. She stared and then opened her mouth and then staggered back several steps into her living room. Burt Roth went first.

"It's okay, KC," he said. "Everything is okay."

Her eyes were wide and she made small noises which were not quite crying. It was as if she couldn't get enough air into her lungs to actually cry. I moved Vincent in ahead of me and Hawk followed us and closed the front door and folded his arms and leaned on it. Talk about theatrical.

KC said, "Burt," in a strangled kind of voice. She didn't look at Vincent.

Roth spoke softly and fast.

"This is kind of like an intervention, KC. People who care about you gathered together to help you get past a hard thing."

"You care about me?"

"Of course. No false messages. Our life together is over, I believe. We each have another life to live. But I've known you most of my adult life. We share a child. Of course I care about you."

She was trying so hard to pretend that Vincent wasn't there that it made all her motions stiff as she avoided seeing him.

"I don't even know that man," she said looking at Hawk.

Hawk smiled at her. When he chose to he could look as warm and supportive as a cinnamon muffin.

"He's with me," I said. "We brought Vincent."

When I said his name it was as if I had jabbed her with an electrode. She winced visibly and looked very hard at her ex-husband.

"What are you going to do?" she said.

"This man raped you, KC," Burt Roth said quietly. "You are too important to let someone misuse you that way."

"You know . . . ?"

"I know he did, KC."

"I never . . ." Vincent started.

Hawk put his hand on Vincent's shoulder and said, "Shhh."

Vincent seemed to freeze when Hawk spoke to him.

"You made a mistake with him, maybe," Burt Roth said. "Everybody makes mistakes. You probably made one with me, too. But they are honorable mistakes. Mistakes made for love. The best kind of mistake to make."

KC was staring at him as if she'd never seen him or anything quite like him. I wasn't sure how much of what he was saying he believed, but he was saying it well.

"And I'm determined," Roth went on, "that you will not have to suffer as you've suffered for making honest mistakes."

"God," KC said, "I have suffered."

"And if we don't put this creep where he belongs." He nodded at Vincent and paused.

I admired how clever he was at avoiding specifics.

"If we don't," Roth said, "will he rape you again? Who else will he rape?"

He paused again, and looked steadily at KC.

"Maybe one day he'll rape Jennifer," Roth said softly.

KC made kind of a moan, and stepped back again and sat down on the edge of her couch as if her legs had given way. Again I believed her sincerity, without missing the contrived quality of it. Maybe she was simply an endless series of contrivances and when they had all been peeled away she could cease to exist.

I said, "Did Louis Vincent rape you, KC?"

She stared at Roth for a time as if I hadn't spoken, then, for the first time, she looked at Vincent.

"Yes," she said.

Behind her eyes hatred crackled, for a genuine moment, like heat lightning.

"Yes he did," she said.

Vincent started to speak, looked at Hawk, and didn't. His gaze shifted rapidly around the room, as if he could find a place to run. He couldn't. I walked over to the end table beside the couch and picked up her phone and called Sgt. O'Connor. Roth sat down on the sofa beside KC. She put her hand out and he took it. Hawk looked at Roth and nodded his head once in approval. For Hawk that was the Croix de Guerre.

O'Connor came on the line.

"Spenser," I said. "We have your rapist if you'd like to come up and get him."

I hung up the phone and turned. Vincent was staring at me. Suddenly his eyeballs rolled back in their sockets and he fell backward. Hawk stepped aside and let him fall against the wall and slide to the floor. He lay on his back with his eyelids open over his white eyeballs and his mouth ajar. We all looked at him.

"Rapist appears a little vaporish," Hawk said.

Faintly I could hear the police sirens coming our way.

CHAPTER FORTY-ONE

I met Robert Walters of Walt and Willie in the late afternoon at a gay bar in the South End near the Ballet.

"Well, the world's straightest straight boy," Walt said when I came in.

He was drinking red wine. And I could tell that he'd been doing it for a while.

"Good to be the best at something," I said.

The bartender had bright blond hair and an earring. The bar had Brooklyn Lager on draught. I ordered one.

"So what you want to talk about, Mister World's Straightest?"

I saw no reason to vamp on the subject.

"I'd like to talk about the blackmail doodle you guys were running with *OUTrageous*."

"Huh?"

"I'd like to talk about the blackmail doodle you guys were running with *OUTrageous*."

"Doodle?"

"You guys were discovering closeted gay people and threatening to out them if they didn't give you money. I'd like us to talk about that."

Walt finished the rest of his wine and motioned to the bartender.

"I'm going to switch to martinis, Tom."

"Belvedere," the bartender said, "up with olives."

"You got it," Walt said.

I waited. Walt watched as the bartender mixed his martini and brought it to him. The bartender put out the little napkin, set the martini on it, and went away. Walt picked up the martini carefully and took a sip, and said "ahh." Then he looked at me, and as I watched him, his eyes began slowly to fill up with tears.

"Whose idea was it?" I said.

Tears were running down Walt's face.

"Willie and I have been together for seven years," he said.

His voice was shaky.

"Long time," I said.

Susan and I had been together for more than twenty, with a little time out in the middle. So I didn't actually think seven was a long time, but it seemed the right thing to say at the moment.

"I never cheated on him," Walt said.

He drank most of his martini and then stared wetly into the glass, twisting it slowly by the stem as he talked.

"And here he is stepping out with Amir Abdullah," I said.

Walt looked at me as if I'd just leaped a tall building at a single bound.

"I'm a detective," I said. "I know stuff."

Walt finished his martini and gestured for another.

"That son of a bitch," he said. "He used to be Prentice's boyfriend, you know that?"

Walt was monitoring the construction of his second martini, and when it arrived he sampled it immediately. He wasn't paying much attention to me.

"So what about the blackmail?"

"Willie and I didn't know anything about it. We were serious about *OUTrageous.*"

He studied his martini again for a time. His face was wet with tears.

"Then when Prentice died, Amir came to Willie and me. He explained what Prentice had been doing. He said that it had a wonderful justice to it, that queers without the courage to come out of the closet could at least be made to contribute to those of us who were loud and proud about it."

"Good to take the high road," I said.

"He said Willie and I ought to continue it," Walt said. "Said that it was a proud tradition."

"He want a cut?" I said.

"No. He said he didn't need the money."

Walt ate the single big olive from his martini, in several small bites.

"Willie loved it," Walt said. "He's always been more rebellious than me. Always ready to give the finger to the straight world."

"What's this got to do with the straight world?" I said.

"During Gay Pride he'd march in outrageous drag," Walt said. "Once he went as a priest with the collar and everything, only wearing a skirt, holding hands with two altar boys."

"That ought to shock them in Roslindale," I said.

"I was always kind of embarrassed by it," Walt went on.

He was having more trouble now, talking, because periodically he'd have to stop and get control of his crying enough to continue.

"Willie used to tell me I was just playing into the straight guilt trap, that I was ashamed of my sexuality. I guess I'm pretty conservative. Willie was always much more out there than old stick in the mud Walt. It's probably why it happened."

He was nearly to the bottom of his second martini. His speech was slurring. I didn't know how much wine he'd drunk before I arrived. Considerable was a fair guess. Right now it was working for me. He was drunk and garrulous and had someone to talk to about his pain. But I didn't know how long I had before he would get too drunk to talk. I wanted to push him, but I had the feeling that if I pushed I'd remind him that he was admitting to a felony and, drunk or not, he might shut up.

"Why what happened?" I said carefully.

"Why Willie started fucking Amir," Walt said and started to cry full out.

The bartender looked at me. I shrugged. The bartender went to the other end of the bar and began to reorganize some clean glasses.

"Who would blame him?" Walt said, snuffling and gulping. "Got this uptight homophobic gay lover. Who wouldn't want somebody more interesting, for crissake. Who wouldn't want somebody with more . . ." He stopped and tried to get his breathing under control. "With more . . . I don't know what, just more."

"I don't know a lot about this," I said, "but I do know that in a situation like this if you can blame yourself it gives you hope. He's out of your control, but if it's your fault, maybe you can fix it.''

"I can change," Walt said.

He had some trouble with the *ch* sound.

"Sure," I said. "You think Amir had anything to do with Prentice going out the window?''

"Amir?''

"Amir Abdullah," I said.

"You mean do I think he killed him?''

He had a lot of trouble moving his mouth from *I* to *think.*

"You could put it that way," I said.

"I . . . I . . . I don't . . ." As he stumbled over his answer, Walt got one of those crafty looks that drunks get when they have this great insight, which in the morning will embarrass them.

"I bet he did," Walt said. "I bet he did an' I bet Willie help' him.''

"Why?''

"'Cause he a sonfabish," Walt said. "They both sonfabish.''

He pushed the nearly empty martini glass away from him and folded his arms on the bar and put his head down on them and mumbled "sonfabish" a couple of times and was quiet.

"Any evidence other than him being a son of a bitch?" I said.

I waited. Walt didn't move. The bartender ambled down the bar. Walt started to snore.

"Walt a friend of yours?" the bartender said.

"No," I said.

"Okay. He's a regular. Bar's almost empty. Let him sleep it off a little. When he wakes up I'll send him home in a cab.''

"Good," I said.

"He's got a forty-three-dollar tab here," the bartender said. "Including your beer.''

I put a hundred-dollar bill on the bar.

"My treat," I said. "Take his cab fare out of that too.''

"Thanks.''

"No problem," I said.

As I was leaving I contemplated the, albeit illusory, sense of power one achieved by slapping a C note on a bar. Maybe I should start carrying several. More important, maybe I should start earning several. At the moment I was doing two pro bonos, one for Susan, one for Hawk. I wondered if it was too late to cut myself in on *OUTrageous*. Maybe I could earn a bonus by telling everyone everything about everybody.

It was raining again, but I was dressed for it, and the walk back up to my office wasn't very far, and I liked to walk in the rain. So I strolled the block down Tremont and turned up East Berkeley with my hands in my pockets and my collar up, while the rain came down gently. I thought about what I knew. I knew a lot, but nothing that solved my problem with Robinson Nevins. It was clearly time to talk with Amir Abdullah again. He almost certainly was a son of a bitch, but he didn't look like someone who could have forced open that jammed window and thrown anyone through it. On the other hand, he might know someone who could.

CHAPTER FORTY-TWO

Hawk and I were parked on Commonwealth Avenue outside the former Hotel Vendome, now a condominium complex. We had decided to conduct our discussions with Abdullah in a different venue, the first discussion having been a little brisk.

"Lives on the fourth floor front," Hawk said.

"Learned anything else about him?" I said.

"Stops by the packie on Boylston, couple times a week, and buys two, three bottles of wine," Hawk said. "Usually before Willie comes calling."

"Anybody else come calling?"

"Almost every day," Hawk said. "Young men. Any race. Look like students. Most of them are one time only."

"You think he's tutoring them in the formulaic verse of the North African Berbers?"

"Be my guess," Hawk said, "that they exchanging BJ's."

"Yeah," I said, "that's another possibility."

"He went away last weekend."

"Where?"

"Took a cab to Logan to one of those private airways service areas, walked out onto the runway, got in a Learjet and . . ."

Hawk made a zoom-away gesture with his hand.

"Came home Monday morning, went to class."

"Private jet?"

"Yep."

"You have any idea where?"

"Nobody I asked knew," Hawk said. "Plane was a Hawker-

Sibley, left at two thirty-five last Friday from in front of the Baxter Airways building. Some numbers printed on the tail.''

Hawk handed me a slip of paper.

"Somebody has to know," I said. "They have to file a flight plan.''

"You know who to ask?" Hawk said.

"Not right off the top of my head.''

"My problem exactly," Hawk said. "I bet Amir will know.''

"Of course," I said. "Let's ask him.''

"He's teaching a late seminar," Hawk said. "Doesn't get home until about seven.''

"Good," I said. "Give us time to break into his apartment.''

"You think he might not let us in if we knocked nice and said howdy doo Mr. Abdullah?" Hawk said.

"I hate your Uncle Remus impression," I said.

"Everybody do," Hawk said happily.

We left the car in a no parking zone and walked across to the Vendome. Hawk said hello to the good-looking black woman at the security desk and pointed at the elevator. She smiled and nodded us toward it.

"Isn't she supposed to call ahead and announce us," I said.

"Un huh," Hawk said.

"Been busy," I said.

"Never no strangers," Hawk said, "only friends you haven't met.''

"That's so true," I said, and pushed the call button for the elevator.

"You know," Hawk said as we were waiting for the elevator, "I suppose Amir got the right to go off on a weekend without us coming in asking him where and why.''

"Absolutely," I said.

"But we going to ask him anyway.''

"Absolutely," I said.

"'Cause we don't have anything else to ask," Hawk said.

"Exactly," I said and got into the elevator.

Hawk got in with me and pushed the button for the second floor.

"You ever think of getting into a line of work where you knew what you was doing?" Hawk said.

"Why should I be the one," I said.

"No reason," Hawk said. "Just a thought."

The elevator stopped. We got out. Hawk pointed left and we walked down the corridor to the end door. I knocked, just to be sure. No one answered. I bent over to study the lock.

"You want to kick it in?" Hawk said.

"Looks like a pretty good dead bolt," I said. "We'll raise a fair ruckus kicking it in."

"Might as well use a key then," Hawk said.

I looked up at him. He looked like he might spit out a canary feather.

"The Nubian goddess at the desk?" I said.

"Un huh."

"You sure you been keeping an eye on Amir all this time?" I said.

"She got a little closed-circuit TV can watch the lobby from her bedroom," Hawk said. "While he in his apartment teaching young men about them formulaic Berbers, I doing a little lesson plan with Simone."

Hawk unlocked Amir's door. We went in. The dark room was close, heavy with the smell of men's cologne mingling with something that might have been incense. I flipped the light switch beside the door. The room was done in tones of brown and vermilion. There was a six-foot African ceremonial mask on the far wall facing us between the seven-foot windows. A squat fertility goddess from Africa's bronze age stood solidly on the coffee table in front of the beige sectional sofa, and a large painting of Shaka Zulu on the wall opposite the sofa. The rugs were thick. The windows along the front were heavily draped. To our left off the living room was a dining area, with a glass-topped table ornamented with two thick candlesticks in tall ebony holders that had been carved to resemble vines. A kitchen L'd off the dining area. The bedroom and bath were to our right. The bed was canopied. On the night table was a small brass contraption for burning incense. On the bureau was a framed photograph of a stern thin-faced black woman with her hair pulled tightly back and her dress buttoned up to the neck.

"Amir got some style," Hawk said.

"Incense is a nice touch," I said.

I sat on the couch. Hawk went over and turned the lights back off.

"Don't want Amir to spot it from the street," Hawk said. "Want him to walk right in and close the door behind him."

He came over, walking carefully while his eyes grew accustomed to the dark, and sat beside me. He put his feet up on the coffee table.

"What's happening with the woman got raped?" he said.

"She's staying with her mother in Providence."

"She getting any help?"

"Susan referred her to a rape crisis counselor, down there," I said.

"She going?" Hawk said.

"I don't know. Her ex-husband said he'd pay for it."

"He likely to end up with her back in his lap," Hawk said.

"I don't think so. I think he's pretty clear about her."

Hawk was quiet for a time.

"'Course there's always your lap," he said.

"Not if I keep moving," I said.

"We got a plan what we do when Amir shows up?"

"We'll ask him a bunch of questions," I said.

"And when he lies to us?"

"We ask him some other questions."

"When do I get to hang him out the window by his ankles?" Hawk said.

"We can always hang him out the window," I said. "Trouble is then he'll say anything he thinks we want to hear, and we may learn as much stuff that's not true as we will stuff that is."

"You just too soft-hearted," Hawk said.

"Softer than you," I said.

"Probably both happy 'bout that," Hawk said.

"This visit we try it the easy way," I said.

"Might stir the pot a little," Hawk said. "Might make him do something that we can catch him at."

"Might," I said.

There was the sound of a key in the door. We were both on our feet. Silently on the thick carpet I stepped into the kitchen, Hawk went into the bedroom. The bolt turned. The door opened. The lights went on. The door shut. I could hear him put the chain bolt on. I stepped out of the kitchen and stood in front of Amir. There was an Asian boy, Japanese was my guess, maybe eighteen years old, with Amir. The moment he saw me Amir spun toward the door. Hawk had stepped out of the bedroom between Amir and the door. Amir turned again and tried for the phone beside the sectional sofa. I stepped between him and it. Amir stopped and looked toward the bedroom. Not a chance. Same with the kitchen. He had nowhere to go. He stood frozen between us. Behind him Hawk took the bolt off, and opened the door slightly.

"You go home," he said to the Asian kid.

The kid looked at Amir. Amir had no reaction. He was stiff with panic.

"Now," Hawk said.

The kid turned and Hawk opened the door enough and the kid went out. Hawk closed the door and put the chain back on.

"Sit down," I said to Amir. "We need to talk."

"Don't hurt me," he said.

Amir's voice was shrill and thin-sounding, as if it was being squeezed out through a small opening.

"No need for hurting," I said. "Just sit down and talk with us."

"The boy saw you here, he'll tell the police," Amir said.

Hawk stepped up behind Amir, put his hands on Amir's shoulders, and steered him to the couch and sat him down.

"Stay," he said.

Amir stayed. Hawk sat on the couch beside him. I sat on a hassock across from them, and rested my elbows on my knees and clasped my hands.

"Now, here's what we know about you. We know it was you who informed the English department tenure committee that Robinson Nevins was sort of responsible for the death of graduate student Prentice Lamont."

"I . . ."

Hawk said, "Be quiet, Amir."

"We know that you yourself were having a sexual relationship with Prentice Lamont before his death."

Amir opened his mouth, looked at Hawk, closed his mouth.

"We know that Prentice was blackmailing gay people who didn't want to be outed, and we know that you knew about that."

Amir sat with his mouth clamped shut, trying to look intrepid, determined to make a virtue of necessity.

"What else do we know?" I said to Hawk.

"We know you a chicken fucker, Amir," Hawk said.

Amir tried to look haughty. He was, after all, a professor.

"I don't even know what that means," he said.

"Sure you do," Hawk said. "Means you'd fuck a young snake if it was male and you could get it to hold still."

Hawk's expression was, as always, somewhere between pleasant and noncommittal. Amir's expression failed at haughty. It was more a kind of compacting silence, as if he was becoming less, dwindling as he listened, freezing in upon himself.

"We know you advised the current staff of *OUTrageous,* namely Walt and Willie, that they should continue the blackmail," I said. "We know you declined to be a financial part of it because you said you didn't need the money. We know you are currently having an affair with Willie, which is causing Walt to refer to you as a son of a bitch."

"And," Hawk said, "we know you went away this weekend in a private plane."

"And here's what we don't know," I said. "We don't know if you made up the story about Nevins, or if it's true. We don't know why you told the committee about it in either case. We don't know why you condoned the blackmail. We don't know why you didn't then take any money from it. We don't know why you claim not to need money. We don't know where you went this weekend. We don't know if you are responsible for Prentice Lamont being dead."

The silence in the thick sweet stench of the living room was palpable.

Hawk said very softly, "We'd like to know."

"I didn't do a thing to Prentice," Amir said.

"Know who did?"

"Prentice killed himself."

"No," I said. "He didn't. Do you know who did?"

"Prentice killed himself," Amir said again.

"Who'd you go to see this weekend?"

"I didn't go anywhere," Amir said.

"You took a private jet out of Baxter Airways at two thirty-five last Friday."

"I didn't."

"We can run that down," I said. "You think people who are gay and don't want the world to know should be announced?"

"There's nothing shameful about being gay."

"I agree. But my question stands."

"Every gay person who announces himself proudly to the world is another step toward full recognition of our sexual validity."

We were beginning to discuss abstractions, and Amir was on firmer ground. His voice was less squeaky.

"Unless they pay off," I said.

"I think of it as a fine for noncompliance," Amir said.

"But you wouldn't take any of the money."

"I do very nicely thank you on my salary and my lecture tours and my writing."

"You have an affair with Prentice Lamont?"

"Prentice and I were lovers. There's nothing wrong with that."

"While he was in love with Robinson Nevins or before."

Amir hesitated. He could sense a pitfall in the question.

"While," he said.

Wrong answer.

"So he was willing to cheat on Nevins but when Nevins left him he was so heartbroken that he killed himself?"

"You don't understand the gay life," Amir said.

"Why do you think Prentice killed himself?"

"Everyone thinks so," Amir said.

"And why did you tell the tenure committee?"

"I felt honor bound to do so."

"Honor bound," Hawk said.

Amir looked at Hawk sort of sideways trying to seem as if he weren't looking at him.

"I know you from before," he said.

"Sure, we come to your office, couple weeks back," Hawk said. "Boogied with some of your supporters."

"No, I mean a long time ago. I know you from a long time ago."

Hawk didn't say anything. His face showed nothing. But something must have stirred in his eyes, because Amir flinched backward as if he'd been jabbed.

I let the silence stretch for a while, but nothing came out of it. Amir was rigidly not looking at Hawk.

"Amir," I said. "I don't believe a goddamned thing you've said."

Amir stared straight ahead. I nodded at Hawk. We stood and went to the door. I took off the chain bolt. We opened it and went out. Before he closed it Hawk looked for a time at Amir. Then he closed the door softly.

CHAPTER FORTY-THREE

I was with Robinson Nevins at the university in the faculty cafeteria, drinking coffee. I was currently experimenting with half decaf and half real coffee. Not bad.

"I met your father the other day," I said.

"Most people are impressed when they meet him," Nevins said.

"He's impressive," I said.

"Hawk's affection for him is sort of touching," Nevins said. "Since, as you must know better than I, Hawk shows very little of anything, let alone affection."

"You like him?" I said.

"He's my father," Nevins said. "I guess I love him. I'm not very comfortable with him."

"Because?"

"Because he is from a different world. Machismo is the essence of his existence, and I am remote from that."

"Is he disappointed in you?" I said.

Nevins looked startled.

"Why I . . . no . . . I don't think he is."

"I don't think he is either," I said.

"You talked about me?"

"Yes. He asked me if I thought you were queer."

"And?"

"And I said I didn't know. And he said he didn't know either, but that it didn't matter much one way or another. You were still his son."

"I knew he wondered," Nevins said. "Forty years old and unmarried."

"I guess the time has come, I need to know," I said.

"If I'm queer?"

"Yeah."

"No," Nevins said. "I'm not."

"Might have saved you some grief if everyone knew that."

"Might have," Nevins said. "But I have always thought that it is entirely corrupt to judge people based on what they do with their genitals in private with a consenting adult."

"I think that's right," I said. "Here's an even worse question. Can you prove it?"

Nevins stopped with his cup half raised to his lips and stared at me a minute, then he put the cup down, and folded his hands and rested his chin on them and looked at me some more.

"Just how do we go about that?" he said. "Go down to the Pussy Cat Cinema, perhaps, see if I erect?"

"Maybe the testimony of satisfied females?" I said.

He nodded slowly, an odd half smile on his face.

"I don't like this much better than you do, but everybody's telling me nothing, and I need some kind of fact to wedge in with."

"What is really, what, ironic, I guess, is that at least one member of the tenure committee knows perfectly well that I'm heterosexual."

"Care to share the name?"

He didn't say anything.

"Look," I said. "It would have to be a female. How many are there on the tenure committee?"

"Four."

"For crissake," I said. "I'm a detective. You think given four names I can't find out which one it was?"

"If I tell you, can you keep it to yourself?"

"I can keep it from anyone who doesn't need to know it," I said.

He still looked at me above his folded hands. The odd half smile faded. Finally he spoke with no expression at all.

"Lillian Temple," he said.

"If that's true," I said, "Lillian Temple knowingly lied about you in the tenure meeting. She was the one who introduced the business about Prentice Lamont.''

Nevins nodded slowly, without taking his chin off his folded hands.

"Was this before she was Bass Maitland's main squeeze?'' I said.

"While,'' Nevins said.

"Ah,'' I said. "And you are too gentlemanly to kiss and tell.''

"That relationship is important to her. I don't want to destroy it.''

"You're getting lynched here,'' I said, "and won't say anything in your own defense because it would be dishonorable.''

Nevins shrugged.

"Honor requires difficulty,'' Nevins said.

"Jesus Christ,'' I said. "Your old man isn't the only one for whom machismo is the essence of existence.''

Nevins widened his eyes at me as he sat there, and cocked his head slightly without lifting it.

"You think I'm motivated by considerations of machismo?''

"I hope so,'' I said. "I hope you're not crazy.''

An old fat black woman in white sneakers shuffled to our table, cleared the table debris, including the coffee cups we hadn't finished, into the cart she was pushing, and shuffled on. Neither of us said anything. I wasn't even sure she had seen us.

"Have you had other girlfriends,'' I said. I wasn't even investigating anymore. I was simply interested.

"Yes, and I've been reticent about them because they have been white.''

"Un huh.''

"And . . . I don't know how to say this without sounding like a priggish jerk.''

"It's okay,'' I said. "You're a professor.''

He smiled sort of automatically.

"Well, I am badly overeducated. I can only relate well to women who are also badly overeducated.''

"And most of those women are white.''

"Yes.''

We were quiet while the old fat black woman came back and wiped off our table with a damp cloth and moved on.

"I'd have thought interracial dating would not have caused problems in your circles."

"I don't know if it would have. I wasn't brought up to believe that it wouldn't. My mother was very careful about staying on *our* side of the line. I find it difficult to overcome my upbringing."

"I've heard that could be hard," I said. "So you kept your dating a private matter."

"Yes."

"And because you were single and forty it was assumed you were gay?"

"Single, forty, educated, bookish, unathletic—do you know I've never played a baskctball game in my life?"

"A clear betrayal of your heritage," I said.

"You know, the funny thing, I have no interest in sex with other men, but I am, in many ways, more at home in the gay community than the straight. I found the gay world readily accepting of a black man and a white woman. No one expected me to be Michael Jordan."

"No one expects anyone to be Michael Jordan," I said.

"You know what I mean."

"Yes, I do. You have a large number of gay friends?"

"Yes. I'm more comfortable in the gay world than I am in the black world."

I wasn't sure that worlds divided themselves so neatly as Robinson suggested, but that wasn't my issue. I nodded encouragingly.

"America expects black men to be macho," he said.

Again, I wasn't sure either of us was in a position to know what America expected, and, again, it wasn't my issue. So I nodded some more.

"Of course," and he smiled suddenly, "I am also refighting the family fight, you know, the refined mother and the father who trained fighters?"

That sounded a little closer to it and I liked him better for knowing it.

"Yes," I said. "Being a straight man in a gay circumstance would be a nice way to do that, wouldn't it."

His eyes widened and he looked at me.

"Well," he said, "you're not . . ." He made a little oh-I-don't-know hand wave.

I finished it for him.

". . . as stupid as I look," I said. "In fact I am. But I have a smart girlfriend."

"I'm impressed," Robinson said.

I went for the complete show-off.

"For a black man," I said, "dating white women might be another way of dramatizing his ambivalence."

"Your girlfriend must have had some therapy," Robinson said.

"She's a shrink," I said.

"Oh," Robinson said, "well, that's not fair."

"Of course not," I said. "I don't like to ask this, but may I speak to your current girlfriend?"

"Yes. Her name is Pamela Franklin. I'll give you her address."

He took a ballpoint pen and a small notebook from his inside pocket and wrote for a moment and tore the page out and handed it to me.

"Thank you. Do you know Amir Abdullah?"

"Yes."

"Comment?"

"Amir is a fraud. He's an intellectually dishonest, manipulative, exploitive charlatan."

"Know anything bad about him?" I said.

Robinson started to protest, caught himself, looked at me a moment, and smiled without much humor.

"You're joking."

"Yes."

"Perhaps you shouldn't so much," he said.

"Almost certainly," I said. "Tell me more about Amir?"

"He has created himself in the image of a black revolutionary, without any vestige of a philosophical ground. I am not by nature a revolutionary or an activist, but I can respect people who genuinely are. Amir is not. He is a contrivance. He gets what he wants by accusing anyone who opposes him of being a racist or a homophobe."

"Or a Tom," I said.

"Yes."

"Are you and he politically opposed?"

"I am not political," Robinson said. "But I disagree with almost anything Amir espouses."

"Have you been critical of him?"

"Yes."

"Would your denial of tenure benefit him?"

Robinson looked thoughtfully at the old fat black woman shuffling among the now nearly empty tables.

"Someone once remarked," he said, "I don't recall who, that the reason academic conflicts are so vicious is that the stakes are so small. There is no genuine benefit to Amir if I am denied tenure. But it would please him."

"And it would reduce by one the number of people who could confront him without the risk of being called a racist."

"Given the number of black faculty members, that would be a significant reduction," Robinson said.

"How about Lillian?"

"What about her?"

"She and Amir are the two members of the tenure committee who told the cops they had direct knowledge of your relationship with Prentice Lamont."

"Lillian?"

I nodded.

"I haven't done anything to Lillian."

"And since we agree that the allegation is untrue, why would she make it?"

"I don't know," he said, "but I could hypothesize."

"Do," I said.

Robinson took in a long breath and let it out slowly. "Most straight black men know someone like Lillian," he said. "She has very little connection to what people outside of English departments sometimes refer to as the real world. She doesn't do things because they would be fun, or they would be profitable, or they would be wise. She does things because they conform to some inner ideal she has structured out of her reading."

"I've met Lillian," I said.

"Okay," Robinson said, and smiled, "a pop quiz: why would you guess she is in this long-term relationship with Bass Maitland?"

"Because he reminds her of Lionel Trilling," I said.

"Or Walter Pater," Robinson said. "You've got the idea. Now, for extra credit, why was she sleeping with me?"

"White woman's burden," I said.

"Yes." Robinson's face was suddenly animated. "And why did she stop?"

"You weren't black enough."

"Wow," Robinson said. "You're good."

"I've met several Lillians," I said. "If she transferred her passions to Amir she could be supporting the aspirations of her black brothers and sisters and still stay faithful to Bass."

"Yes, and I'm sure that's what happened because that was what she thought she was doing. But she'll be unfaithful to Bass again."

"Because what she really liked was the sex?" I said.

"As long as she could disguise it under a mound of high-mindedness."

"My guess is that Bass is not Lionel Trilling."

"No," Robinson said. "He's just your standard academic opportunist blessed with a good voice and nice carriage."

"We might have saved a lot of time and aggravation," I said, "if you'd told me all this at the beginning."

"Or if you'd asked," Robinson said.

I nodded. "Both had the same reasons, I guess. Can you prove you had a relationship with her?"

"Obviously I can't prove I, ah, penetrated her. I've got some pictures of us together."

"I'd like the best one of you both," I said. "You meet any-place where there'd be a witness?"

"Witness?"

"Did you check into a motel, have drinks together in Club Cafe? Spend the night at a friend's house on the Cape?"

"We spent several nights together at a little place in Rockport that is hospitable to black people."

"What's the name?"

"Sea Mist Inn," Robinson said.

"When's the last time?"

"We went up there last Labor Day weekend. Last time we went out."

"Thank you."

"I don't want to cause her trouble," Robinson said.

"Me either."

We were quiet then. The old fat black woman had shuffled out and we were alone in the empty dining room.

"You know," Robinson said after a while. "My father named me after Jackie Robinson."

"No one better," I said.

"I know. I guess I've always felt I never lived up to it."

"Nobody's Jackie Robinson," I said. "You're doing pretty well."

"I wish you were right," he said.

"I'm always right," I said. "I have a smart girlfriend."

CHAPTER FORTY-FOUR

I was asleep when my car blew up. The sound of it woke me, and I got to the window in time to see some of the fragments land on Marlborough Street. Aside from the post-explosion fire, there was no activity on the street. I looked at my watch, 3:35 in the morning. I couldn't think of anything to do about my car. I didn't see a felon fleeing the scene. But I was too wide awake to go back to bed, so I stood and watched. In about ten minutes a police cruiser pulled up Marlborough and halted near the now declining embers where once my car had been. I got dressed and went down, and announced myself as the owner. While I was talking with the cops, the fire department arrived and then a couple of arson investigators, and my night was shot.

When I got to my office about ten in the morning, less rested than I was used to, there was a message on my machine to call Captain Healy at State Police Headquarters.

"Plane you were asking about," Healy said when I got him. "Private plane owned by an outfit called Last Stand Systems, Inc. Flew from Logan to Bangor, Maine."

"Do you know anything about Last Stand Systems?"

"No."

"Got an address for Last Stand Systems, Inc.?" I said.

"Beecham, Maine."

"That's it?"

"That's it," Healy said. "You ever heard of Beecham?"

"No."

"Me either."

"It's a wonder you got promoted to captain," I said.

"No wonder at all," Healy said and hung up.

I got out my atlas and looked up Beecham. It was on the coast, southeast of Bangor. I called the office of the Maine Secretary of State in Augusta and, after a while, learned that Last Stand Systems, Inc. was a not-for-profit corporation. After another while, I got the names of the principal officers, and the members of the board. According to their incorporation papers Last Stand Systems was committed to social and political preservation. After I hung up I looked at the list of names. None of them meant anything to me. The CEO was somebody named Milo Quant.

I called information and asked for Last Stand Systems, Inc. and got it. I called them and asked for literature. They asked my name and address. I told them I was Henry Cimoli and gave them the address of the Harbor Health Club.

Then I called Henry and told him to look for the literature and asked him to have Hawk stop by. Which Hawk did in about an hour. There was always something lustrous about Hawk. His shaved head gleamed. He moved as if he were spring loaded. And there was about him a kind of genial absence of affect that made him seem almost otherworldly.

"I think we might have buzzed somebody's button," I said. "My car blew up last night."

"Trying for you?" Hawk said.

"I don't think so. It went off at three thirty-five in the morning, a guy who could have rigged that device wouldn't have gotten the timer so far off."

"Want to kill you he ties it to the starter anyway," Hawk said.

"Yes. But there's no way to know what I'm being warned about, yet."

"So they going to have to follow up," Hawk said.

"Un huh. Call me, write me, come and visit me."

"They'll come calling," Hawk said. "Show you they can reach you whenever they want."

"Yes," I said, "and see how I take the warning."

"You talk to anyone since we sat with Amir?"

"No."

"So maybe talking with Amir was the buzzer."

"Maybe. Or maybe busting Louis Vincent was the buzzer, and they just got around to following up."

"Nope," Hawk said, "this a warning. Too late to warn us off Vincent."

"Yeah," I said. "You're right."

"Who that plane belong to?" Hawk said.

"Last Stand Systems, Inc.," I said. "Out of Beecham, Maine."

"Beecham, Maine?"

"I never heard of it either," I said.

The door to my office was open so that Hawk and I could keep an eye on Lila in the design office across the hall. Six men in close formation came through the open door like a drill team. Two moved to the left of the door, two to the right, and two marched straight up to my desk.

"Maybe these guys know," Hawk said.

"You guys know where Beecham, Maine, is?" I said.

They looked like Secret Service men or IBM executives. They were all in dark suits and white shirts. They all wore ties. They all had short hair. They all were of northern European descent. When everyone was in place the suit closest to the door pushed it shut.

One of the two men in front of my desk said, "Spenser?"

He was wearing horn-rimmed glasses, which made him look smart, probably why he was the designated speaker.

"Yes," I said. "Is it on the coast?"

"Is what on the coast?"

"Beecham."

Horn Rims shook his head in dismissive annoyance.

"You've been put on notice," he said. "As of this morning at three thirty-five."

I looked at Hawk.

"Did you take those library books back like I told you?" I said.

Hawk was leaning against my file cabinet as if he might fall asleep. He smiled softly.

"Can't be librarians," Hawk said. "Librarians would know where Beecham is."

Horn Rims didn't change expression.

"You are to stay entirely away from Amir Abdullah. Repeat,

entirely. If you fail to comply you will be incinerated as was your car.''

"How come," I said.

"You've been informed," Horn Rims said. "Your Negro friend as well.''

"You guys associated with Last Stand Systems?" I said.

One of the guys in the back opened my door, and four of them marched out. Horn Rims and his partner marched out after them. At the door, Horn Rims' partner turned and aimed a semiautomatic pistol with a silencer. He squeezed off three rounds; each shot broke one of the three coffee cups that were lined up on the file cabinet about a foot from Hawk. Hawk never moved. The gun disappeared. The door closed. We were left with the silence and the smell of the gunfire.

Hawk looked at the remains of the coffee cups.

"Guy can shoot," Hawk said.

"Yes, my Negro friend, but is he a nice person?" I said.

FORTY-FIVE

The pictures of Lillian and Robinson arrived in my office by FedEx. I took them with me when I drove up to the Sea Mist Inn and talked with the homey-looking woman at the desk. She remembered them clearly enough, a black man and a white woman. They had registered as Mr. & Mrs. Robinson Nevins on the Friday before last Labor Day, and, yes, that was Mrs. Nevins in the picture.

I drove back to Boston and over to the university and took the information and the pictures with me. I fell in beside Lillian Temple as she came down the steps of the library carrying her briefcase. She appeared to recognize me, but she didn't appear to take any pleasure in it.

"Hi," I said.

"I'd prefer that you did not bother me while I'm at work," she said.

"Don't blame you," I said. "You know anything about the Sea Mist Inn?"

"Excuse me?"

"Sea Mist Inn, place up in Rockport where you and Robinson Nevins spent last Labor Day weekend."

She stopped dead in the middle of the quadrangle.

"Labor Day?"

I took the photographs from my inside pocket.

"I showed these pictures of you and Robinson," I said. "And the woman on the desk recognized you."

She stared at the photographs.

"This came on you kind of sudden," I said. "Should we sit on this bench, while you think about it?"

Without comment, she plopped down on a bench beside some evergreen bushes near the entrance to the administration building. She was staring at the pictures I still held for her.

"Those pictures don't prove anything," she said finally.

I put them back into my inside pocket.

"No, but they're suggestive, coupled with what the Sea Mist lady told us, and what Robinson Nevins said."

Again she was silent, staring at the place where the pictures had been. She let out a long breath.

"Well," she said, "you seem to have invaded my whole life."

"Just doing my job, ma'am."

Lillian looked at me somberly.

"Not a job one can admire," she said.

If Lillian had a sense of humor, I had no idea how to access it.

"So," I said. "Since we can assume you know Robinson Nevins was heterosexual, a question presents itself."

Lillian continued to look at me with blank sobriety, which might have been her attempt to look stern. Lillian's mind didn't seem to move very quickly, even for a professor. While the question had come upon her rather suddenly, it was a pretty obvious question. I waited.

Finally she said without affect, "What question?"

"Why you reported to the tenure committee a story about Robinson Nevins that you had considerable reason to doubt."

"He could have been bisexual."

"Yes he could have. Did you think he was?"

"I didn't know he wasn't."

"Did you ask him?"

"Of course not." She was, maybe genuinely, outraged. "One's sexuality is neither my business nor yours."

I looked at her for a while, aware of my breath going in and out.

"It's breathtaking," I said. "You have ruined a man's career by repeating a slanderous allegation you know to be false, and you still find a way to mouth moralistic platitudes when you're caught."

"I'm sorry you think the right to privacy is a moralistic plat-
itude."

"I am also not sure if you know that you keep diverting the
topic or not. I don't think you're smart enough, but now and
then I'm fooled."

She stood, holding her briefcase with both arms, as if I'd tried
to cop a feel.

"I do not have to sit here and allow you to berate me," she
said.

"No you don't," I said. "And neither will the Dean of Liberal
Arts, when I discuss it with him."

She sat back down again, hugging her briefcase a little closer.

"You'd go to the dean?"

"Yep. Probably go to Bass Maitland, too. And probably the
student newspaper."

She was horrified. The look of haughty incomprehension had
been replaced by wide-eyed staring fear.

"I want a lawyer," she said.

"Sure," I said. "Go get one. I'm not a cop. You're not under
arrest. But I now know that Robinson Nevins got jobbed in his
tenure hearing, and I know by whom, and I can prove it, and I
will. What I don't know yet is why, but I'm not sure *why* matters."

The class break had ended and the next period had begun. The
quadrangle was relatively empty. Some students sat on the library steps smoking, and listening to headphones, and talking
and thinking about sex. In the small plot of dirt where the ev-
ergreens grew by the steps of the administration building, some
tough-looking city birds, starlings mostly, and a few sparrows,
pecked industriously for whatever birds peck after. In front of
the university, MBTA trains stopped and let people out and took
people on before they tunneled back underground.

Finally in a voice that sounded almost girlish Lillian said,
"You wouldn't understand."

"Probably not," I said.

She took her left hand off her briefcase and began to play with
the hair at the back of her neck.

"A university faculty is special. It is a place, maybe the only
place, where the ideal of a civil society still flourishes."

"I can see that," I said.

If she heard me she didn't show it.

"Robinson is a decent man, but he . . . he has no place on a university faculty. He is not . . . how to say this . . . he is not consistent with the current best thinking on racial matters."

"How is he at teaching English?" I said.

"That's a fallacy. A university faculty is not simply about teaching, it is about creating and passing on culture. The university is a place where the best minds must be allowed freedom to contemplate the most basic human issues. A university faculty is the progenitor and propagator of culture."

I was certainly glad I had said "by whom" a while ago.

"Would you say Robinson is out of step with current racial thinking in the sense that he does not see it as genocidal to teach dead white men in his classes?"

"That's part of it, though of course you would put it in a way that makes it sound puerile."

"So you felt obligated to lie about him to the tenure committee because he was not the right kind of black guy," I said.

"Again you have demeaned my point," she said.

"Someone ought to," I said. "I'm glad I could be the one."

"I did what I thought best in the larger context."

"Let me get one thing clear," I said. "This bastion of civility you've been speaking of, is Amir Abdullah a tenured member of it?"

"Yes."

"I refute it thus," I said.

She came out of her abstraction trance enough to look puzzled.

"Is that a quote?" she said.

I couldn't stand her anymore. I stood.

"Samuel Johnson," I said. "Look it up."

I left.

CHAPTER FORTY-SIX

Unless I am under actual attack, I always read the paper in the morning while I drink coffee. If I'm away I read whatever morning paper is local. When I'm home I read the *Boston Globe*. So when Henry dropped off the literature from Last Stand Systems on his way to work on Tuesday morning, I put it aside until I had drunk my third cup of coffee and finished the comic section. Then I folded the paper back up and put it aside in case I wanted to consult it later. Sometimes "Doonesbury" was too hard for me the first time through and I had to reread it later.

The stuff from Last Stand Systems was obviously computer-generated, though it was pretty professional-looking with colors and right-justified margins and typefaces that someone had thought about. It was also dreck. The centerpiece of their promotional literature was a newsletter titled *Alert!* which warned against the encroaching mongrelization of the white race, the feminization of the American male, the homosexual assault on marriage, the debasement of American Christianity, and the arrival of the Antichrist. There was a thoughtful discussion, complete with footnotes and bibliography, of a secret plot which festered deep within the power centers of the federal government, abetted by Zionism, whereby this country would be handed over to the One Worlders at the UN. The author signed himself Octavio Smith, Ph.D. The writing was grammatical and wooden.

I put *Alert!* down and picked up the other stuff. There was a letter from the CEO, Milo Quant, explaining that Last Stand's mission was to restore the America our fathers had founded. There was also an application for membership, and a calendar of upcoming Last Stand events. I filed the application which required a $100 fee and looked at the calendar. It was mostly a list of Quant's public appearances. The closest one was at the state college in Fitchburg, Mass., Friday night, sponsored by a student group. A don't-miss opportunity.

Last Stand Systems, Inc., seemed the most unlikely organization to be flying a black homosexual radical activist named Amir Abdullah up to Maine for the weekend. But they had, and there was no plausible explanation that I was able to come up with. It was also possible that they had sent out a squad of well-scrubbed shooters to chase us away from him. Again I couldn't think why. Maybe they were using him as a recruiting ploy. Enough exposure to Amir Abdullah would make anyone a racist homophobe.

My office door opened. It was Susan. She had a small bag of Key lime cookies she'd bought somewhere and wanted to share them with me over coffee. Sharing meant Susan ate most of one cookie, and I ate all the rest in about the same amount of time. I had no problem with that.

"There's a fund-raiser at the ART Friday night," Susan said. "I'd like us to go."

She had put the cookies out on a little paper plate and was making coffee.

"Oh darn," I said. "I have to drive out to Fitchburg State and listen to a speech by a racist homophobe."

"Well," Susan said, "I couldn't ask you to give that up. Decaf all right?"

"Sure," I said. "Want to can the ART and go with me?"

I watched her as she spooned the coffee into the filter. She always made it too weak.

"Yes," she said, "but I can't. I'm on the board, you know. I just hate to go alone."

"Bring Hawk," I said. "He's got a good sense of humor."

"Oh my," Susan said.

We were silent for a moment, both of us thinking about Hawk at the fund-raiser.

"Whyn't you add another heaping spoonful of coffee," I said.

"Won't it be too strong?" she said.

"No, and a pinch of salt."

"Okay," she said and did what I said, although I could tell by the set of her shoulders that she knew the coffee would be salty and much too strong to drink. She turned on the coffee-maker and stood looking down at it while it began to brew.

"I'm missing you," she said while she watched.

"Yeah, I'm missing you, too."

"I feel like we haven't seen enough of each other," Susan said.

"Working couples," I said.

"Do you think we can get away soon, just the two of us, somewhere?"

"Yes," I said. "A mystery ride?"

"I'd love that," Susan said.

"I'll put something together for us."

"I don't want to tour the new ballpark in Cleveland," Susan said.

"And you don't want to go to Cooperstown," I said, "and visit the Hall of Fame."

"That still leaves a lot of options for us," Susan said.

"I guess so," I said. "I wonder if KC Roth would like to see the Hall of Fame."

"She's probably in it," Susan said. "They probably retired her diaphragm."

"Her diaphragm?"

"I'm an old-fashioned girl," Susan said.

"And not a jealous bone in your body."

"Not one," Susan said.

The coffee had brewed enough to fill two cups. Susan poured it and put the pot back, added milk and Equal, and brought the two cups to my desk.

"Why are you going to listen to a speech by a racist homophobe?" she said.

"His name popped up in the Robinson Nevins case."

"Really."

I was on my second cookie. Susan had a small bite out of hers. The coffee was just right. I knew she thought it was just right too, but wasn't saying so because she was stubborn.

"Last weekend a plane came to Logan and picked up Amir Abdullah and took him up to Bangor. The plane belonged to

Last Stand Systems, Inc., of Beecham, Maine, and this speaker
is the CEO of Last Stand Systems, Inc., which appears to be at
the far right end of the family values movement.''

"Is that being put kindly?" Susan said.

"Very," I said. "We asked Amir about this. He denied that
it happened."

"So what will you learn by going to the speech?"

"Don't know," I said. "See what this guy looks like. Hear
what he sounds like. Maybe I'll get to ask him about Amir.
Mostly I don't know exactly what else to do, so I'm going to
do that. You know, keep looking until I see something."

"I know very well. We do somewhat the same thing in therapy."

We finished our cookies and drank our coffee.

"Coffee's just right," I said.

"I thought it was a little strong," Susan said, "and a tad
salty."

I grinned at her. I got up and walked around my desk and
stood in front of her.

"I love predictable," I said. "Will you give me a big lingering open-mouthed kiss?"

Susan patted her lips with a little paper napkin that had been
in the bag with the cookies. She stood.

"Yes," she said. "I will."

CHAPTER FORTY-SEVEN

I got a call at my office the next morning from KC Roth inviting me to lunch. I figured I was safe in a public place, so I accepted. We met at the Legal Sea Foods restaurant in Chestnut Hill, and because we were early we didn't have to wait long.

"I've moved back into civilization," KC said, when she was seated across from me with a glass of white wine.

"Chestnut Hill?" I said.

She shook her head.

"Not enough dollars," she said. "Place in Auburndale, the first floor of a nice two-family."

We looked at menus and ordered. KC had another glass of white wine.

"I . . . I have to say things," she said.

"Okay."

"I . . . I'm sorry about some of the crazy things I did. Calling you up and leaving you notes."

"No harm," I said.

"I was just . . . crazy, I guess. Crazy time, you know?"

"I know."

"And of course I want to thank you for saving me."

"Just had to convince you to save yourself. Your ex-husband was more useful than I was."

"Yes. Burt was there for me. Sometimes I think I made a mistake. I could be there now in a nice house with someone taking care of me."

"You can take care of yourself," I said.

"I didn't do much of a job of it before," she said.

"Your ex-husband send you money?" I said.

"Alimony."

"Enough?"

"Enough to be independent," KC said.

"Or dependent."

"Sure, men always say things like that. You have no idea what it is like to have been a married housewife forced suddenly to take care of herself."

"You're right," I said.

She sipped her wine. The restaurant was busy. Legal Sea Foods are always busy.

"You think I should get a job?" she said.

"I think if you supported yourself and didn't take money from your ex-husband, in the long run you'd feel better about things."

"I wonder if he's seeing anyone."

I didn't say anything.

"He was there for me," KC said.

"And he urged you not to misunderstand," I said. "He reminded you that you and he had different lives to live."

"Of course you'd stick up for him. Men always stick up for each other. The old boys' network."

"I'm not so old," I said.

"Oh pooh," she said. "You know what I mean."

The waitress brought chowder for KC and lobster salad for me. KC took the opportunity to order another glass of wine. We each had a taste of our lunch. KC's wine came and she had some.

"But," she said, "I didn't ask you to lunch to complain."

"Oh," I said.

"I just wanted the chance to let you know that I understand how much you've done for me."

"My pleasure," I said.

"Is he-whose-name-shall-not-be-mentioned going to be in jail a long time?"

"Ask me after his trial," I said.

"What if he doesn't go to jail?"

"He will."

"But what if there's, you know, a miscarriage of justice?"

"Then we'll take the necessary steps," I said.

"You'll still be there for me?"

"It's sort of what I do, KC."

"But I haven't even paid you."

"I know."

"What if he comes back and I still can't pay you?"

"We'll work it out," I said.

"I . . . I just don't think I can cope if I don't know you're there."

"Where?" I said.

"You know, there for me."

"As I said, that's sort of my profession."

"You mean you're there for anyone who hires you."

"More or less," I said.

She was taking in more wine than chowder, which was a shame because the chowder at Legal was very good. I finished my lobster salad.

"When you were sitting by my bedside," KC said, "after the . . . that awful thing happened to me, I thought maybe I might be more than just someone who had hired you to be there."

I didn't like the way this conversation was going.

"Part of the service," I said.

She put her hand out and placed it firmly on top of mine, and stared into my eyes.

"God damn it," she said, "can't you see I love you?"

I felt like I'd wandered into a remake of *Stella Dallas*.

"I don't think so," I said. "I rescued you from a bad situation. And you need to be in love with someone to feel secure and you don't have anyone else to love at the moment, and I'm handy and you think I'm it."

"Don't tell me what I feel," she said.

"Are you still seeing the therapist Susan recommended?"

"Drive all the way to Providence twice a week to talk about my father? I don't think so."

"Susan can get you someone up here."

"You think I'm crazy?"

"I think you need help in figuring out who to love and who to trust and what you need."

"Talk talk talk. Why can't men ever simply feel?"

"You need help in not generalizing, too," I said.

She stood up so suddenly that she knocked over her empty wine glass. She came around the table and threw her arms around me and kissed me on the mouth. I sat stock still feeling like a virgin under siege. Flight seemed unbecoming. KC was pushing the kiss as hard as a kiss can be pushed. I remained calm. When she broke for air she leaned her head back and stared into my eyes some more.

"I love you, you bastard," she said. "Don't you understand that I love you."

"If you don't let go of me," I said, "and sit back down, I will hit you."

She straightened up as if I actually had hit her, and stared at me, and began to cry. Sobbing loudly, she turned and ran from the restaurant. Everyone in the place watched her leave, and then looked at me with either disapproval (almost all of the women, some of the men) or sympathy (several of the men, one woman). My waitress remained unperturbed. She brought me the check.

CHAPTER FORTY-EIGHT

The post office in Beecham, Maine, was located in one corner of a variety store in a small weathered-shingle building at the top of a short hill which led down to the harbor. The coast of Maine was tourist country, and a lot of shopkeepers had adopted a kind of stage Yankee persona in order to fulfill expectations.

"I'm looking for Last Stand Systems," I said.

The shopkeeper/postmaster was a fat old guy wearing a collarless blue and white striped shirt, and big blue jeans held up by red suspenders.

"In town here," he said.

As he answered me he eyed Hawk. The look wasn't suspicious exactly, it was more the look you give to an exotic animal that has unexpectedly appeared. The way he might have looked if I'd come in with an ocelot on a leash.

"Where in town?"

"Out the Buxton Road," he said.

"Does it have an address?" I said.

"Beecham, Maine."

The shopkeeper was seated on one of four stools bolted to the floor in front of a marble-topped soda fountain, his fat legs dangling, his fat ankles showing sockless above a pair of moccasins. There were donuts under a glass dome, and straws and napkins in chrome dispensers.

"Does it have a number on it?" I said.

"Nope."

"If I went out the Buxton Road how would I recognize it?"

"See the sign out front."

"The one that says Last Stand Systems, Inc.?"

"Yep."

"That should help us," I said.

"Might."

"How do we get to the Buxton Road?" I said.

"Right out front. Turn right."

"You been working on this act for a long time?" Hawk said.

The old fat guy almost smiled for a moment, but fought it off and stayed in character.

"Yep," he said.

"Real hay shakers wear socks," Hawk said.

"Some do," the old fat guy said.

Hawk grinned. We turned and went back out and got into Hawk's car and turned right. Nearly all the houses were white and set on low foundations. Many had long porches that wrapped around the front and one side where people could sit in rocking chairs and look across the street at people sitting in rocking chairs looking across the street. The Buxton Road barrel-arched over a fast-moving little river and then flattened out between tall pines on the right and the sea-foamed boulder-scattered coastline on the left. The sea birds seemed livelier on this coast. There was very little of the effortless gliding that gulls did in Boston. Here, they flashed above the waves, and dove into the foam, and scooted over the rocks and snapped food out of the tidal ponds that formed among the rusty-looking granite chunks. About a mile out of town there was a narrow drive off into the pine trees. A small sign, black letters on white wood, read Last Stand Systems, Inc. Hawk U-turned and pulled up onto the shoulder at the opposite edge of the road above the ocean fifty yards down past the sign.

"We could be bold," Hawk said.

"And if it's the outfit that sent the well-dressed shooters," I said, "we could be dead."

"Or, we could be guileful."

"Guileful?"

"Guileful."

"I vote for guileful," I said.

"Good," Hawk said, "what you suggest?"

"You don't have a plan?"

"I come up with the strategic concept," Hawk said.

"Is that what that was?" I said. "I thought you were just showing off you knew a big word."

"That too," Hawk said.

"Okay, let's sneak around in the woods and see what we can see."

"Covertly," Hawk said.

"Of course," I said. "Covertly."

Hawk and I were both in work clothes, which meant jeans, sneakers, tee shirt. I wore a blue oxford dress shirt with the tails out to hide the Browning on my belt. Hawk mostly used a shoulder holster. To conceal it he was wearing a gray silk sport coat. He took it off and folded it carefully on the backseat. He had a big .44 Mag under his arm.

"Doesn't the weight of that thing make you tip to the side?" I said.

"It do," Hawk said. "But you never know when you might have to shoot an elephant." Hawk put the car keys over the visor.

"Case we need wheels real quick," Hawk said. "Don't want to be looking for the keys."

"'Course this could be an outfit of pleasant people who make umbrella stands," I said.

"With an unlisted number and a private jet," Hawk said.

"Just a thought," I said.

We crossed the road and went into the woods. It had that bittersweet scent that the woods often have on a hot day. Except for the whine of locusts, and the occasional movement of the wind off the ocean, it was very still. Pine needles were six inches thick underfoot. We made very little sound as we walked. We walked in a wide circle aiming to come to Last Stand Systems, Inc. from a direction other than the road. It was easy going. There was very little underbrush. It was as if the land beneath the high pines had been carefully cleared. In about twenty minutes we saw the compound. Not much to see. It looked like it might once have been a manufacturing facility that had been recycled. There were three cinder block buildings with those high glass windows that nineteenth-century industrial buildings used to have, the kind that have a fine wire mesh running through them. The buildings were painted flat white. The compound was surrounded by a high chain link fence with razor wire on top.

I climbed a tree. From there I could see that the buildings faced onto an open area about the size of a football field. An American flag was on a flagpole in front of one building. A couple of men in dark suits and white shirts came out of the building by the flagpole and walked across the open area and went into the building across the way. I looked down. Hawk had taken a seat under the tree with his back against the trunk and his ankles crossed and appeared to be asleep, though he probably wasn't.

I sat in my tree some more. There's something about sitting in a tree when you're a grown man that makes you feel like a doofus. But it was a feeling I understood, I'd had it before. I sat, doofus-like, and looked at the layout. To my left was a gated entrance with a guard shack manned by a guard. The gate was open, folded back out of the way against the chain link fence. The central building with the flagpole was directly opposite the gate. It was clearly the administrative place. The suits continued in and out of there. The other two buildings seemed to be a barracks and maybe a supply warehouse. A couple of green Jeeps and a black Lincoln stretch limo with tinted windows were parked in front of the administration building. They all had Maine plates. I noted the plate numbers.

As I watched, a man in starched fatigues and wearing a pistol belt strolled slowly along the fence. There was a radio on his belt on the hip opposite the pistol, and a microphone clipped to his epaulets. At the corner he stopped and spoke to another guy with the same equipment who had obviously walked down his length of fence. One of them leaned his hand against the chain link as they talked. Which meant the fence was not electrified. The other two lengths of fence were hidden by the buildings. I watched as my guy turned smartly and strolled back along his fence and, sure enough, met another guard at the other corner. Being a trained observer I concluded that the perimeter was guarded by four men. I watched some more. The guards went back and forth. After about a half hour a squad of four other men in starched fatigues came out of the far building under the direction of another guy and they marched out to change the guard. I sat some more. In the next hour and a half I counted at

least twenty men in starched fatigues and sidearms either guard-
ing the perimeter or marching about in the compound in something resembling close order drill. My left knee was beginning
to hurt where I'd gotten shot once. I wasn't sure I could stand
the excitement of another guard change, so I climbed back down
the tree and stood and stretched out my knee a little. Hawk tilted
his head back and looked at me.

"So, Hawkeye," he said. "What'd you see."

"Looks like something between an IBM retreat and Parris
Island," I said.

"Got a perimeter guard," Hawk said.

"I counted about twenty guys in fatigues and sidearms," I
said.

"Don't seem necessary for a bunch of pleasant umbrella stand
makers," Hawk said.

"No," I said. "It doesn't."

"We tough enough to go in there and roust twenty guys?"
Hawk said.

"Of course we are," I said.

"How 'bout stupid enough?" Hawk said.

"Sure, but then what? I don't even know what we're looking
for in there."

"Same thing we looking for when we drove way the fuck up
here," Hawk said. "We trying to figure out the connection between Amir and this outfit."

"Oh yeah," I said. "And we're doing that because we think
it might help us figure out who threw Prentice Lamont out the
window."

"Exactly," Hawk said.

"Shooting it out with twenty guys may not be the best way
to get that information."

"Specially if only one guy's got the information and you kill
him."

"A definite possibility."

"Or we might both get shot to pieces and then the thing
wouldn't ever get solved," Hawk said.

"Unlikely," I said. "But not impossible."

We both looked at the gleam of the white cinder block buildings through the lacy distraction of the trees. The high locust
whine was so much a part of the woods that it had become nearly

inaudible. The bittersweet smell of the woods was stronger as the sun had gotten higher.

"I think guile is still our best option," I said.

"So what the guileful thing to do?" Hawk said.

"Go back home, maybe have a couple beers, and think about it," I said.

"Works for me," Hawk said.

CHAPTER
FORTY-NINE

Heading back to the car we were maybe twenty yards from the highway when we both stopped short at the same time.

"You smell it?" I said.

"Cigarette," Hawk said.

I nodded. Hawk took his elephant gun from the shoulder holster and stuck it into his belt at the small of his back. He shucked off the shoulder rig and dropped it and moved off to the right. I went left. We emerged onto the highway bracketing the car, Hawk ten yards beyond it, me ten yards this side. There were four of them leaning on the car. They had on uniforms and carried side arms. An unmarked blue Jeep was parked behind Hawk's Jag. I sauntered toward them with a big friendly smile.

"Hi," I said. "You waiting for me?"

One of them turned toward me. He was still wearing his horn-rimmed glasses and it still made him look smart. Of course, appearances can be deceiving.

"This your car?" he said. After he said it, he stared at me and I could see recognition begin to form behind his lenses.

"Actually it belongs to my Negro friend," I said.

They had not planned on being approached by two people at the same time from opposite directions. They should have divided the chore. Two look at me. Two look at Hawk. But they hadn't decided in advance, and therefore didn't know, which two should look at whom. Training is good, but sometimes innovation is better.

"I know you," Horn Rims said.

"And a better man for it," I said.

Hawk and I kept coming. Horn Rims put a hand on the radio at his belt and turned his head and spoke something into the microphone clipped to his epaulets. Then he unsnapped the flap of his holster.

"Stop right where you are," he said.

"Here?" I said.

For a moment all four of them were looking at me. When two of them looked back at Hawk, he had put the car between him and them and was resting the big .44 on the roof with the hammer back.

One of them said, "Jesus Christ" and all four looked for a moment at Hawk. When two of them looked back at me I had the Browning out and cocked and pointed.

"You guys got to be better organized," I said. "Move away from the car."

Horn Rims glanced toward the driveway. He was expecting reinforcements. I stepped closer and hit him with a left hook that staggered him into the road. Then I got in the car and fumbled the keys down from the sun visor. Hawk remained with his gun on the security guards.

"You're a dead man," Horn Rims screamed at me. "Wherever you run, whatever you do, even if you kill some of us, we'll run you both to ground and kill you."

From up the long driveway I could hear the sound of cars coming. More than one. I started the Jaguar.

I heard Hawk say, "Watch this."

There were two big booms from the .44 and in the rearview mirror I could see the Jeep settle forward on its rapidly deflating front tires.

I heard Hawk say, "All of you on the ground, facedown."

Then Hawk was in the front seat. I stomped on the accelerator and the Jag lunged forward spinning up gravel from the road shoulder. We lurched up onto the road surface and screeched away. I could smell the tires scorching and there was some small-arms fire, but nothing hit us. Hawk slammed the door shut as the car stabilized and smoothed out.

"We going to have to do something about these guys," Hawk said.

I was driving as fast as the Buxton Road would let me back

toward Beecham. Hawk had the cylinder of his .44 open and was feeding in two fresh rounds that looked about the size of surface to air missiles.

"I'll bet they're back there saying the same thing," I said.

CHAPTER FIFTY

I had the mystery ride all put together. Until I figured out exactly what Hawk and I were going to do about Last Stand Systems, Inc., I wanted the time I spent with Susan to be covert. I was in a profession where getting threatened was part of the deal. So was Hawk. But Susan was not. So I left Hawk to look out for himself for a long weekend and took Susan for a few days to Lee Farrell's empty condominium at Sanibel Island on Florida's west coast. It was late June, and as out of season as you could get. But I was pretty sure no one would shoot at us while we were down there.

It was all right on the plane, and in the car rental office, and the car we rented was air-conditioned. The walk from the car to the elevator and the ride up in the elevator was not air-conditioned, and we were near collapse by the time I got Farrell's door unlocked. The condo was roasting. It had been closed since Farrell's last vacation. I staggered to the thermostat and turned the air-conditioning on high. In a few minutes the crisis had passed and we were breathing normally again.

"I don't want to disappoint you," I said to Susan after she had unpacked and hung up all her clothes and joined me at the little bar in the living room for a cocktail. "But Farrell made me promise there would be no heterosexual carnality in here."

"Is this your way of telling me you want me to dress up in a man's suit again?" Susan said.

"Lee says it's in the bylaws of the condo association—heterosexuality is prohibited."

"Oh boy," Susan said. "Finally a real vacation."

"Gee," I said. "Usually when someone tells you that you can't do something, you want to do it immediately."

Susan sipped on the Bellini I had made her and looked at me and frowned thoughtfully.

"You know," she said, "you're right. That is how I am. The hell with the condo association. Let's fuck."

"That's the Susan I know," I said. "Did you say something about a man's suit?"

"Just a little humor," she said.

"How about maybe just the shirt and a tie," I said.

"Stop it," Susan said and got up and walked toward the bedroom. I followed.

"How about just the tie?" I said.

Susan unzipped her shorts.

"How about less talk and more action," she said.

LATER THAT NIGHT we had dinner at The Sanibel Steak House. The dining room was small and pleasant with glass at the far end looking out over some greenery. We both had martinis. They were excellent. We both ordered steak. For Susan to order steak was a breach of self-discipline comparable to masturbating in public. Salads arrived first. They were excellent. The steaks arrived shortly thereafter. Susan recovered herself sufficiently to cut her steak into halves and put one half aside.

"I guess we showed them," Susan said as she chewed on a small piece of steak. "Sex, martinis, and steak. How much more carnality is possible."

I took a bite of my steak. It was excellent.

"That can be our project while we're here," I said. "See how much carnality is possible."

"Would you care to tell me exactly why we are here?"

"Haven't been away in a while," I said. "Lee offered."

"Lee's a cop," Susan said. "He doesn't spend all winter here either. Why now at the end of June?"

"Sure it's out of season," I said. "But everything's air-conditioned."

"I'm not complaining about the heat," Susan said. "And so far I'm having a lovely time. But I think that there's something lurking behind the arras."

"A rat, maybe?"

"Or Polonius," Susan said. "Shakespeare aside, I know you nearly as well as you know me. What's up?"

I finished my martini, and in a burst of unbridled carnality, Susan finished hers. The waitress noticed our situation and came over. We ordered red wine. She went to get it. And brought it back and left.

"You remember Beecham, Maine?" I said.

She shook her head. I told her, all of it. She listened as I talked as she always did, with full attention, her eyes fixed on me. I could feel the charge in her. I could feel the energy between us. It made talking to her a lush experience.

"And you obviously believe them," Susan said when I finished.

"That they'll try for Hawk and me? You remember Clausewitz on war?"

"I should," Susan said, "by now. You keep quoting him."

"And what is the quote?"

"Something like 'you must prepare for the enemy's capability, rather than his intentions.' "

"Yes."

"So you have to assume they might try."

"If I assume they might try and I'm wrong, I'm inconvenienced. If I assume they won't try and I'm wrong, I'm dead."

"Which is why you brought me here. Because if we were to spend time together you wanted it where I wouldn't be in danger by proximity."

"Yep. I figure they follow us down here in late June and their bullets will melt."

"And you still don't know their connection with Amir?"

"Only that they sent a plane for him. And warned us away from him."

"It's the first time in this case that you've run into people who seem like they could have killed Prentice Lamont," she said.

"Yeah, I noticed that too. Don't know if they did, but at least we can assume they would."

Susan had another bite of steak. I sipped some red wine. I had finished my steak and was keeping track of what happened to the half of her steak that she had put aside. It was still aside. I remained hopeful.

"So what are you going to do?"

"Keep pushing," I said. "Something will pop out."

"The police can't help you?" Susan said.

I shrugged.

"We say they threatened us, they say they didn't, what are the cops going to do?"

"You wouldn't go to the police anyway," Susan said. "And certainly Hawk would not."

I didn't say anything. Susan put her knife and fork down, and folded her hands under her chin and gazed at me in silence.

"Don't let them kill you," Susan said.

"I won't," I said.

She thought for a minute, looking at me, and then said, "No, you won't, will you."

"No."

We sat and our eyes held like that for a long minute.

Finally I said, "You going to eat the rest of that steak?"

She kept staring at me and then began to smile and her eyes filled up, and then she began to laugh and the tears spilled onto her cheeks.

She managed to say, "No."

"Good," I said.

I forked the steak onto my plate and sliced off a bite.

"Do you have a plan for tomorrow?" Susan said.

She had herself back under control but her face was still flushed the way it gets when she cries, or laughs, or both, and there was still some wetness on her completely sensational cheekbones.

"I thought we could sleep late, have a leisurely breakfast, once again defy the condo association for much of the afternoon, have a swim and go for dinner at a place called the Twilight Cafe. I hear they have a steak with black beans that you won't be able to finish . . ."

She was laughing again. There was a slivered edge of fear behind the laugh, but it was real laughter.

"As I think about it," she said, "I don't think anything can kill you."

"Nothing has," I said.

CHAPTER FIFTY-ONE

We were lifting weights at the Harbor Health Club. Hawk in a tank top is a fairly scary sight, and a number of the other patrons glanced at us covertly from time to time. Hawk knew this. He never missed anything going on around him, and while, as usual, he paid no attention to anyone, I think it amused him. Now and then he would do something showy like handstand push-ups, to impress the rubes.

"While you been vacationing," Hawk said, "I been detecting."

"Good," I said. "You can use the practice."

"Every Friday Amir go up to Bangor. Every Sunday he come back. So I figure I better see what he doing up there, and I drive up to Bangor International Airport . . ."

"International?" I said.

"Sure," Hawk said. "You think they hay shakers up there?"

"Well," I said. "Yes."

Hawk shook his head. He was doing some dips as he talked, and if there was any effort involved it didn't show in his voice.

"Anyway, I'm there on a Friday afternoon sitting in my car, and about five o'clock here come Amir out of the terminal with his little overnight case. Black Lincoln stretch limo waiting. Driver gets out, opens the door. Amir hands him the overnight case, driver puts it on the front seat, Amir hops in the back. You want to guess the license number on the limo?"

"Don't remember but I'll bet it's in my notes."

"Same one," Hawk said.

"You follow them?" I said.

"Yep."

"To Beecham."

"Yep."

"Last Stand Systems, Inc."

"Yep."

"Stayed the weekend and came home Sunday night."

"Yep."

"You got any theories on what he's doing up there?" I said.

"Visiting."

"You got any thoughts on what he does while he visits?"

Hawk was doing pull-ups. He did five more after I asked the question, then let himself down slowly and dropped to the floor.

"We know Amir is queer."

"Nice rhyme," I said.

"And we know he, ah, hyperactive."

"Nice phrase," I said. "You think he's got a boyfriend in Last Stand Systems, Inc.?"

"Somebody send the company plane down for him."

"You think it's Milo Quant?"

"There a Mrs. Quant?" Hawk said.

I didn't say anything for a minute.

"You think there's hanky-panky between Milo and Amir?"

"Amir was a white woman, what would you think?" Hawk said.

"That there was hanky-panky between Milo and Amir."

Hawk smiled.

"That what I'd think," he said.

"So," I said. "We don't want to be homophobic about this."

"So hanky-panky it is," Hawk said.

"On the other hand," I said, "you've read the literature. For the leader of this movement to be having an affair with a gay black militant is not just miscegenation, for crissake, it's treason."

"You right," Hawk said. "Couldn't happen. Be like J. Edgar Hoover running around in a dress."

"Exactly," I said. "Impossible."

I did some curls. Hawk worked on his triceps a little. I did some dips. Hawk worked on his lats. Henry strolled past us and explained to someone that the leg extension machine gave you a better workout if you put some weight on it. He showed them how to set the weight, then he walked back past Hawk and me without looking at us.

After a while Hawk said, "I feelin' short on electrolytes."

"Me too," I said. "Luckily Henry keeps some in his office."

We went back into Henry's office that looked out over the harbor and got some beer out of the refrigerator.

"Milo is speaking out in Fitchburg," I said. "I thought I'd go out and listen."

"Why?"

"Why not? Right now I got so little that knowing what he looks like will help."

Hawk nodded.

"I had a lover in Maine," he said, "and he coming to Fitchburg, maybe I arrange to meet him."

"Why don't you stick with Amir," I said. "And I'll tag along behind Milo Quant. And we'll see."

"Say we catch them doing the hoochie coochie," Hawk said. "What we got?"

"More than we got now," I said.

"That much," Hawk said.

"Well, we've got some stuff," I said. "We've already got Amir connected to an outfit that is capable of pitching someone out a window."

"True."

"What we don't have is proof that they did it, or any reason why."

"Prentice a blackmailer," Hawk said.

"Could be a reason," I said.

"Don't forget why we doing this," Hawk said.

"I know. Robinson's tenure," I said. "I think we've got enough now. But it's messy. I want it clean."

"How often you get clean?" Hawk said.

I grinned.

"Figure I'm due," I said.

CHAPTER FIFTY-TWO

I was getting ready to drive out to Fitchburg when KC Roth called me on the phone.

"I'm sorry about the other day," she said.

"Un huh."

"I guess I'm a little crazy right now."

"Probably."

"It's not easy being me, you know."

"I know."

"I'm alone, I have no prospects, I need support. I guess sometimes I get a little too aggressive."

"Nothing wrong with aggressive," I said. "But you need to focus it properly."

"Easy for you to say. You're not alone."

"The question isn't whether it's easy for me to say. The question is am I right?"

"I didn't call up for you to give me advice," KC said.

"No," I said. "Of course you didn't."

"It's frankly none of your goddamned business."

"It was," I said. "But now it isn't."

"That doesn't mean I can't call you up and have a civil conversation, does it?"

"No it doesn't," I said.

"Well fine," she said and slammed the phone down.

I seemed to be in a lovers' quarrel with someone who was not my lover. I hung up the phone and looked at it for a moment and then got up and went to get my car.

Fitchburg is a little working-class city of 40,000 people about fifty miles west of Boston. It is also south of Ashby and southeast of Winchendon and north of Leominster, and a great many people don't care much where it is. The state college is up the hill from Route 2A. There were signs directing me to the evening's event. When I got to the auditorium there were several Fitchburg Police cars and at least three blue and gray State Police cruisers parked around the place, taking all the best spots. I parked in a slot that said *Faculty Only*, and walked over to the auditorium. There were cops in the lobby, cops at the entrances, standing around talking to each other. There were also several Ivy League–looking guys in shirts and ties and dark suits, clustered near the main entrance door, scanning the crowd. One of them was the guy with the horn-rimmed glasses who had come to my office with his associates and spoken unkindly to me and Hawk about Amir Abdullah. He had also spoken even more brusquely to us in Beecham, Maine. I had the impulse to step into his line of sight and say, "booga, booga," but I was there to observe, and I usually observed better if no one was paying any attention to me. I went in another entrance, and took a seat in the back. The room was full. Mostly students. From their conversations I gathered that not all of them were fans of Milo Quant. At 7:30 Horn Rims and his fellows walked out quietly and stood at parade rest on the floor of the auditorium between the front row of seats and the stage. I noticed that there were state and local cops along the walls on both sides of the auditorium. A heavyset woman in a pale blue pants suit came onto the stage and stood behind the lectern. She waited for a moment and when she saw that the audience wasn't going to quiet, she began.

"I'm Margaret Dryer," she said. "I'm the dean of student affairs here. Like many of you present I do not agree with Mr. Quant's view of the human condition."

The audience quieted a little as she spoke.

"But I agree with his right to hold those ideas and indeed to espouse them, however repellent I personally find them to be. That is the meaning of free speech, and I hope each and every one of you in the audience will respect Mr. Quant's right to free speech. There has been talk of disruption. I have heard it, just as you have heard it. The police are here. We have asked them to be here. We have asked them to protect everyone's right to civil discourse. We have also asked them to prevent any infringement on those rights, and they will do so."

She paused for a moment. The audience was quiet. Then she turned and gestured toward the wings of the stage.

"May I introduce our guest, Mr. Milo Quant, of Last Stand Systems, Incorporated."

The audience booed the minute his name was mentioned. The booing magnified when he strolled out from the side and replaced Dean Dryer at the lectern. He stood silently for a time, smiling down at the audience, allowing the roar of boos to roll over him. He was a short fat man in a well-made blue suit, a white shirt, and a maroon silk tie. It was hard to be sure from where I sat, but his shoes looked as if they had lifts in them. His nose was sharp and curled a little at the tip like the beak of a falcon. His mouth was wide with thick lips. His face was fleshy. He had thick eyebrows that V-ed down over the bridge of his nose. His upturned smile was V-shaped so that he looked sort of like a devilish Santa Claus. The boos continued. He stood quietly smiling. After a while the students tired. The boos dwindled. Finally it was nearly quiet.

"There," Quant said. "Feel better?"

There was some more booing, but there was also a scatter of laughter. Quant beamed down at us.

"There, I'm not such a monster now am I? Look a little like your grandfather, maybe."

Somebody laughed. Somebody yelled "Fascist."

"Do you know where the word *fascist* comes from?" Quant said.

He leaned slightly forward at the lectern, so that his mouth was closer to the microphone. He let his folded hands rest quietly on top of the lectern.

"It comes from ancient Rome. It derives from the word *fasces* which refers to the symbol of Official Power, a bundle of reeds with an axe head protruding. We at Last Stand are hardly fascists. We don't symbolize official power. We oppose it. We oppose a government hell-bent to dissemble my country, your country, our country. We oppose a government which will make us not Americans, but mongrelized members of a world government where every Arab despot and cannibal dictator may say yea or nay to us."

He was good. The audience was listening.

"And we ask you to join us in that opposition. We are not asking of you the sacrifices that were asked of the men who founded this country."

"And women," someone shouted.

Quant smiled.

"They made their own sacrifices. But I'm talking about the men who were asked to fight and often die for liberty. We don't ask that of you. We ask only that you keep yourself worthy of the liberty they died for. We ask that you keep yourself clean and straight. We ask that you value marriage. That you respect the God of our fathers. That you honor your ethnic purity. That you fulfill the destiny for which so many of those men suffered and died."

He paused. They listened. He smiled warmly at us all.

"If this be treason," he said slowly, "let us make the most of it."

Some people clapped. A few hooted. Most were quiet. Quant went on. If he spoke ill of other races and religions, if he said that all American values were to be found only in white Christian males, he said it obliquely, sliding it in always in terms of honor and cleanliness, heritage, straightness, and respect.

He spoke until 8:15, and then took questions. The majority of the questions were hostile. He handled them easily. He had heard them before. He never said nigger, or queer, or Jew, or dyke. He managed also to be more magnanimous than his questioner, and he always had a gracious and convincing answer for even the most difficult questions.

His answers were largely bullshit, but they were good bullshit. I had years ago learned that it was useless to debate zealots. They had spent most of their adult life thinking intensely about the object of their zealotry. Normally their debaters had not. I wanted to stand and ask him if in fact he were wearing lifts in his shoes. But I was there to watch and listen and I didn't want to get into it with Horn Rims or any of the other preservers of our heritage. So I shut up. Which is a ploy that often works well for me.

When it was over, Quant was escorted out by his keepers and the cops. It was raining. A small group of students were standing across the street, getting wet, chanting "Two, four, six, eight,

USA can't use your hate." I wondered why protesters so often demeaned their deepest-held convictions by reciting them loudly in doggerel. Nobody in Quant's party paid any attention to them. And, in fact, neither did many people in Quant's audience. Shielded by an umbrella one of the security guys deployed, Quant got into his black Lincoln and departed with three body-guards. The other security guys got into a large van. The protesters chanted at them until they were out of sight. Then they stood somewhat aimlessly for a few moments and then drifted away in various directions.

I suspected that Quant hadn't convinced anyone who hadn't come convinced. But he had made them see that he was pleasant, and that he spoke as if what he espoused was both reasonable and kind, and they were puzzled. And maybe they didn't enjoy doggerel much, either.

My car had a parking ticket on the windshield issued by the Fitchburg State College Campus Police. I took it off my windshield and tucked it carefully under the wiper of the car next to me. Then I got in and drifted along behind Quant with the windshield wipers making long steady sweeps across my glass, their sound like the rhythm of music that wasn't playing.

CHAPTER
FIFTY-THREE

At about 10:30 with the rain coming down steadily, the Quant limo pulled off of Route 495 near Chelmsford and into the parking lot of a big motel that looked like the Disney version of a Norman castle. The van kept on going. I followed Quant, and got into a slot in the next row and watched as Milo and his bodyguard deployed umbrellas and walked across the glistening parking lot into the hotel lobby. The place was more hotel than motel, in that it was four stories high and entry was through the front door. For my purposes, I would have liked the conventional one-room one-door approach, but the more I live the more I don't always get what I want. I sat for a while and thought. While I was doing this Hawk opened the passenger door and slid in, the rain beaded on his smooth head.

"Ah ha!" I said.

"Ah ha indeed, my good man," Hawk said. "The game's afoot."

"Amir," I said.

"Yowzah," Hawk said. "Rents a car this afternoon, comes out here 'bout three o'clock. I see him pull in and I take a chance and get into the lobby 'fore he do. There a phone booth right by the desk. I'm in it with my back turned and the phone at my ear when he gets to the desk. He's got a reservation. He's in room four seventeen."

"Good to know," I said.

"Well, I got nothing much else to do so I hang around, sit in the bar, read a paper, drink some Perrier with a nice wedge of

lime, have a club sandwich, drink some more Perrier and about
five minutes ago in come a group of people and one of them is
our man with the horn-rimmed glasses. They got reservations.
Their rooms are four fifteen and four nineteen.''

"Either side," I said.

"Un huh."

"There were four bodyguards, right?"

"Including the limo driver," Hawk said.

"Plus Quant."

"Two bodyguards in four fifteen," I said. "Two bodyguards
in four nineteen. Where's Quant go?"

"Four seventeen," Hawk said. "Want to take a look?"

"Sure," I said. "Why don't I register and we can look at the
room setup."

"Call from the car," Hawk said, "make sure they have a
room."

I did. They did.

"Okay," I said. "Stay here. I'll call you."

I left the motor running, took a gym bag from the trunk of
my car, and walked toward the lobby. The gym bag looked right,
but all it contained were burglar tools. I checked into the lobby.
They gave me room 205. I went up and let myself in and put
the gym bag on the bed and called Hawk.

"Room two-oh-five," I said.

"Fine. Is the desk clerk a man or a woman?"

"Woman."

"Good. I'll come in tell her I'm Amir and I've lost my key."

"They often want to see ID," I said.

"She'd be scared to ask me," Hawk said. "Scared I say she
racist for asking."

"And if she remembers Amir at all it'll be that he's black and
so are you, so you must be him."

"Un huh."

"See you soon," I said.

And I did. In about ten minutes he knocked on the door and
I let him in. He smiled at me and held up the plastic key card.

"She thought I look like Michael Jordan," Hawk said.

"You know how to play that old race card," I said. "Don't
you."

"I do," Hawk said.

The room was standard B-class hotel. Tile bath and shower in the short hall as you came in the door, king-sized bed, small table and two chairs by the window, built-in bureau with a large television set on top of it. The door unlocked electronically with the plastic card and could be chain bolted from the inside. I looked at the chain bolt. The chain was attached to the door frame by two small brass screws. I took a small pry bar from the gym bag.

"Bolt the door," I said.

I took the room key and went out and shut the door. I heard Hawk set the chain bolt. I opened the door with the plastic card, slid the pry bar in through the opening, and popped the chain loose without much effort. I went back into the room and closed the door.

"Shouldn't be hard getting in there," I said.

"Once we in what we going to do?"

"I guess we'll ask them what they're doing here," I said. "And then we'll see what happens."

"What you want to happen?"

"I want everyone to get so percolated that they start saying things they will later regret and we might finally know something concrete."

"And what we going to do they start hollering and the bodyguards come dashing in?"

"I thought you had that covered," I said.

"'Course I got it covered," Hawk said. "I just meant you want me to shoot them or quell them with a stern look?"

"Stern look will probably cause less ruckus," I said.

"I'll work on it," Hawk said, and we went out and took the elevator to the fourth floor.

CHAPTER FIFTY-FOUR

The room was half lit by the security lights that shone on the parking lot. We could have kicked the door in while singing Verdi's "Othello" and neither Milo nor Amir would have heard us. They were in bed together, zonked. Hawk walked over to the bed and leveled his gun at them. When he was in place I closed the door, found the light switch, and turned on the lights. They slept on. Amir was on his side, his back to Milo who lay on his back, his mouth half open, snoring gently. Hawk put the big Magnum back under his coat. He picked up the telephone from the bedside table and disconnected the handset and tossed it onto one of the soft chairs by the window table. There were dirty dishes on the table, remnants of food, glasses, and an empty champagne bottle. There were also five small plastic pill bottles, the kind prescriptions come in. I picked one of them up. It had no label. I took off the top. It contained five large maroon capsules. I dumped them out on the table. I picked up another one. Blue capsules. All five were unlabeled. All five contained some sort of pills. I dumped all of them out on the table.

"Recognize any of these," I said to Hawk.

He shook his head.

"Only do booze," Hawk said. "But they don't look like prescriptions."

Milo opened his eyes. They didn't focus. His mouth was still open and he was still making soft snoring noises. Hawk took his gun back out. Milo blinked a couple of times. He closed his mouth. He blinked a couple more times. Then he sat bolt upright and as he did so Hawk put the gun muzzle right up to Milo's face.

"Don't yell," Hawk said.

Milo fumbled at the bedside phone. He couldn't find the handset and couldn't seem to register that it was gone.

"Phone won't work," Hawk said.

"There's money in my wallet," Milo said in a thick voice. "In my pants pocket. On the back of that chair."

"Wake him up," I said and nodded at Amir.

Milo turned and shook Amir awake. He came back from wherever he was even more slowly than Milo had, but after a while everyone was awake and looking at each other.

"Tell Milo who we are," I said to Amir.

Both men had edged up into a sitting position, their backs resting against the headboard. Both were half covered by the bedclothes. Both their upper bodies were naked. Amir wore three thick gold chains. His chest was black and bony. There was a lot of short curly hair on it. Milo had no jewelry, nor hair on his chest. He was fat and pale with blotchy pink highlights.

"They're," Amir paused, "the white one is a detective."

"Detective? Damn you, you have no right . . ."

Hawk tapped him gently on the forehead with the muzzle of his gun.

"Shh," Hawk said.

"Tell him what detective I am," I said.

"What detective? I don't know what . . ."

"I'm the detective you sent your people to threaten," I said.

"Threaten?"

I knew that Milo's brain was fuddled by whatever controlled substance he'd been ingesting with Amir. But even so he looked genuinely puzzled.

"Didn't he do that, Amir?" I said.

"I . . . how would I know?"

"Well, you and Milo seem sort of friendly," I said. "I just thought you might. So, tell him what we're doing here."

"Doing here? God, how would I know?"

"You know," I said. "Explain to Milo what we're after."

"Speak up, Amir," Hawk said.

Amir looked as if someone had taken a shot at him.

"They're after me," Amir said. "They are after me because they think I made a person lose tenure."

"Tenure?" Milo said.

"And because a kid you know got pitched out a window," I said. "Tell him about that."

"Window?" Milo said.

"It's all craziness, Milo," Amir said.

Milo looked at me and Hawk. Rallying is hard when you're half stoned, and you got no pants on, but Milo was trying.

"There are armed men in rooms on either side of us," Milo said. "If you were to fire that revolver, they would rush in here and kill you."

Hawk smiled.

"You think?" he said.

Milo turned his head and stared at Amir.

"What is this about tenure and a person getting thrown from a window?"

"It's not anything, Milo."

"What are you doing to me, you degenerate cannibal?"

"Who are you calling degenerate?" Amir said. "I'm everything you hate and you can't stop fucking me."

Milo slapped him across the face. Amir laughed at him.

"Talk about degenerate," he said.

It came all at once. Gestalt. The whole thing. For the first time since Hawk had come in with Robinson Nevins in the spring, I knew what was going on. It was a feeling I wasn't used to.

"Prentice knew about you and Milo," I said to Amir.

Amir's face seemed to freeze.

"You got a lot of perks out of being a militant black man, just like you got a lot of perks out of being a militant gay activist."

Milo had stopped looking at Amir and was looking at me.

"And Prentice caught you," I said to Amir.

He seemed to be freezing right there in front of me. Compacting as he froze, growing smaller.

"Who, pray tell, is Prentice?" Milo said.

"Kid that got thrown out the window by some of your security twerps," I said.

"I know nothing about any Prentice."

"No," I said, "you don't. Prentice Lamont ran a newspaper

called *OUTrageous*, which was primarily committed to outing gay men and women who would have preferred otherwise."

Milo frowned. I knew he could identify.

"First the kid probably was doing it for philosophical reasons. Hiding one's sexuality contributed to the belief that it was shameful. Something high-sounding like that, but then, and I'm guessing here, Amir started hitting on him, and the kid was flattered because Amir is a big-deal gay guy and a leading black activist, and a professor, and an all-around joy to contemplate."

Outside the room the rain kept coming down in the dark. The motel window was streaked with it.

"And Amir gives him the blackmail idea. Maybe he wanted a cut of it. Maybe he wanted Prentice to think he was smart. Maybe he gets a kick out of perverting idealism. I'd guess all of the above with the perversion of idealism especially appealing to him, because he did it again with Willie and Walt when he was with you, Milo, and no longer needed the money. There's people like that, get a kick out of seducing virgins, so to speak."

Both Milo and Amir were now watching me as if I were Scheherazade. Hawk seemed to have faded back a little into the background. No one made a sound. I was talking mostly to Milo now.

"Anyway the scheme was working good. Good enough for Prentice to have accumulated two hundred fifty thousand dollars. Also, while Amir was with Prentice, he learned that *OUTrageous* was investigating the possibility that another professor at the university, Robinson Nevins, was gay. Nevins was Amir's bitterest rival, and Amir filed that away for future use."

The pupils in Amir's eyes seemed to have reduced to pinpoints. I spoke to him again.

"But somewhere in there you got bored with Prentice, and you dumped him and moved on and somewhere in there you took up with Milo Quant."

Neither of them said anything.

"And Prentice was jealous, wasn't he?"

Amir shrugged, as if he were embarrassed to talk about how magnetic he was.

"And he used his *OUTrageous* sources and he found out who you'd left him for."

"The damned queen used to follow me," Amir said to Milo.

Milo was looking at him as if he had just discovered a Gila monster sharing his pillow.

"And that was too explosive to let out," I said. "Each of you sexually involved with everything you hate. Hard as it is for me to imagine it, I assume you have devotees, and your devotees would be hysterical. It would ruin both of you."

Milo's face was mottled to an almost maroon flush. Amir was rigidly still. It was raining harder outside. The water flooded down the motel window in crystalline sheets.

"So you spoke to one of the bodyguards, the guy with the horn-rimmed glasses, maybe, and they went and threw Prentice out his window, and left a generic suicide note, and went back up to Beecham."

"I . . ." Milo Quant's voice was very hoarse, it sounded as if it was squeezing out of a very narrow opening in his windpipe. "I knew nothing of this."

"No," I said. "You probably didn't. Amir probably said that you wanted it done and didn't want to know about it. Was it the guy with the horn rims, Amir?"

Amir stood up suddenly from the bed. He was naked. Hawk moved slightly to his right between the door and Amir.

"Chuck," Milo said. "Did you have Chuck kill this boy?"

Amir stood looking around the room. He seemed unaware that he had no clothes on.

"Up to there, he'd probably have gotten away with every-thing, and you and he could have waltzed to the music of time for the rest of your lives. But he got greedy. He put out the story that the boy had killed himself because of Robinson Nevins. That way he gets rid of the kid, and he gets rid of a man whom he saw as a threat to his position as boss black man at the university. And that brought Robinson's father in. And he brought Hawk in. And Hawk brought me in and here we are."

"Is this true, Amir?" Milo wheezed.

"No. No. No."

"You can consult with Chuck," I said. "See what he says."

Amir broke for the door.

"Let him," I said to Hawk. "How far can he get?"

Hawk smiled and Amir Abdullah, naked, burst out of the room and disappeared down the corridor.

On the bed, Milo began to blubber. I could pick out the train of his complaint at first.

"I fought it," I think he said. "I fought it day and night . . . but it consumed me . . . it is my sin . . . my corruption. I gave in to my corruption. And it has brought me to this."

The ratio of blubber to clarity diminished so quickly as he continued that the rest seemed all blubber and I couldn't understand it.

"What I think we need here now," I said to Hawk, "is some cops."

Hawk grinned and went to the chair and picked up the handset and reattached it to the phone. I took it and called the cops while Milo sat in the bed with his face in his hands and sobbed.

CHAPTER
FIFTY-FIVE

Pearl was visiting for the day. She and I had some donuts while I read the paper, and around 10:30 in the morning I put her leash on and took her for a stroll. As we walked down Boylston Street, I realized that I had picked up a tail. By the time we crossed Arlington Street I realized that the tail was KC Roth. I crossed Boylston at the light and went into the Public Gardens. I let Pearl off her leash so she could point pigeons and barrel fruitlessly after squirrels. KC came behind me. I thought about what to do. Pearl spotted a duck and went into her full point, elongating her body, sucking up her stomach, one paw raised, head extended, tail motionless. I stopped beside her and aimed my finger at the duck and said ''Bang'' loudly. The duck flew up a few feet and resettled near the small bridge. Pearl seemed satisfied and began tracking Devil Dog crumbs among the shrubs.

KC was still behind me. I could confront her. I could lose her. Or I could ignore her. It was Wednesday. Susan didn't see patients on Wednesday. She taught a seminar Wednesday mornings and took Wednesday afternoon off. It was our day to have lunch together. I smiled—a solution had presented itself. Pearl and I strolled and KC stalked us until we got back to the office at 11:30. Pearl and I went up. Pearl drank some water and then flopped on the rug. I stood and looked out my window. KC had taken up a position across the street outside F. A. O. Schwarz where she could gaze up at my window. I felt like the Pope.

Susan was due at noon. She arrived of course at 12:20.

''Sorry, sorry, sorry I'm late,'' she said.

"It's okay," I said. "You're always late. I expected you to be late."

She came over and gave me a large kiss, which, I thought, boded well for later. When she was through kissing me she went directly to the mirror over my washbasin and began to reapply lip gloss.

"Where shall we lunch?"

"We could go straight to my place," I said.

"Un uh," she said. "And eat about four in the afternoon?"

"We could order out," I said.

"Sure, and while we waited . . . ? I don't think so."

"Where would you like to go?" I said.

"Anyplace where you won't try to undress me."

"You're the one that came in here with the big kiss," I said.

"Because I love you, does that mean I have to lie down im-mediately on my back?"

"I think so," I said. "Though I've never been a stickler for position."

"I've noticed," Susan said. "Let's go to the Ritz Cafe."

"Sounds good," I said.

I smiled to myself.

"Why are you smiling."

"Just happy," I said.

We walked Pearl down to my place and put her in my living room. I put fresh water in Pearl's dish, and turned on the radio so she'd have music to listen to. She hated talk radio. Susan kissed her good-bye, and we went out. We came back out of my apartment and turned left on Marlborough Street and right on Arlington.

"Talk to me a minute about people who stalk people," I said.

"Sure," Susan said. "I suspect you know what I know. It is some sort of attempt to maintain or, I suppose, acquire the feel-ing of power over someone. Following a person may not give you real power, but it gives you the feeling of it. You watch them. You know where they go, what they do, who they see."

"Knowledge is power," I said.

"Exactly," Susan said.

"Are stalkers dangerous?" I said.

"Not necessarily. Sometimes the need for power extends to

physical coercion, sometimes not. Sometimes dirty tricks, sometimes not.''

"And the purpose?"

"Fear of loss," Susan said. "A lover, say, from whom you
are estranged. You fear if she gets out of your power you'll lose
her. And the feeling of power is a way to feel as if you haven't.''

We were at the corner of Commonwealth less than a block
from The Ritz when Susan spotted KC Roth. She stopped dead
in her tracks and stared at her. KC realized that Susan had seen
her and tried to look as if she were just strolling along and didn't
notice us.

"What the hell is this?" Susan said to me.

"The lovely and tenacious KC Roth," I said.

"She's stalking you again?"

"Yep."

"You knew it?"

"Yep."

"And you didn't say anything?"

"I thought it would be more dramatic if you discovered her
yourself.''

"It is," Susan said.

She was quiet for a moment, then she turned toward KC Roth
and yelled.

"KC!"

KC tried to look startled.

"Susan?"

"Get over here," Susan said.

KC walked over to us.

"Susan, what are you . . . ?"

"Shut up," Susan said.

She jabbed at a bench on the mall.

"Sit down," she said.

Her teeth were clenched and her face was hard-edged and kind
of white except for red splotches on her cheekbones. I stood a
few feet away. *Oh boy!*

KC wasn't brave, but she was stupid. She stood there looking
at Susan.

"Wha . . . ?" she said.

Susan took hold of her blouse with both hands and yanked
her to the bench and slammed her onto it.

"Now listen, you asinine little shit for brains," she said with her teeth clamped hard together. "This is the last time you bother him, you understand?"

"Bother?"

Susan still had hold of her blouse. She pulled her close for a moment and slammed her back against the bench.

"Call, follow, whine at, see, talk to, touch, look at, annoy, anything—you understand? Annoy him again and I will knock out every stupid fucking tooth in your stupid fucking mouth."

KC began to cry. She twisted loose from Susan and stood up.

"I need him," she screamed at Susan. "You have no right to keep him from me, if it weren't for you . . ."

With her clenched fist Susan hit KC on the jaw with a left hook just like I'd taught her, getting her shoulder into it so that the power came from the body, not the arm. KC fell backward and sat down hard on the bench. Her lip was bleeding.

"Are we clear?" Susan said.

KC touched her mouth and took her hand away and stared at the blood on it.

"My God, I'm bleeding," KC said.

"You'll be sleeping with the fishes, you neurotic bitch," Susan said, "if you don't stay away from him."

KC nodded, still staring at the blood on her hand.

"Say it," Susan said with such force that I was a little scared.

"I'll stay away."

"You bet you will," Susan said.

She turned and looked at me and said, "Come on," and started off toward The Ritz at a very fast pace. I followed her. We went in the Commonwealth Avenue entrance and across the lobby into the cafe. The maître d' put us in a window seat only a few inches from passersby on Newbury Street.

"My hand hurts," Susan said.

I nodded.

"You didn't tell me that it hurts your hand to hit someone."

"Mostly," I said, "if you hit them on the face or head. It's why I try to use my forearm or elbow when I can."

"I'll try to keep it in mind."

"Were you influenced by Freud or Adler," I said, "when you gave KC a whack on the kisser."

"Wonder Woman, I think. Not very shrink-like, was I."

"No."

"Did you mind?" Susan said.

"No. I liked it," I said. "It was what I wanted to do, but felt I couldn't."

"You knew I'd blow my top," Susan said.

"I was hoping," I said.

"What do you think she'll do?" Susan said.

"Dash back to the shrink you sent her to, that she stopped going to."

"So she can report me," Susan said.

"Yep."

Susan smiled.

"So maybe it was just the right thing to do," she said.

"I'm sure it was. Will your reputation be destroyed in the psychiatric community?"

Susan smiled again, more broadly than before.

"No, my colleagues will envy me."

"Good," I said. "Want to see if they'll bring you some ice for your hand?"

"No, but they'd better rush a martini out here pretty quick," she said. "Before I'm overcome with pain."

I signaled the waiter.

"Right away, Mrs. Silverman, I sure as hell don't want to cross you."

The drink came promptly, and a beer for me.

"You think it worked?" Susan said. "You think she'll leave you alone?"

"Oh, I'm sure it will," I said. "But you better not let word get out about my sexual performance, or you'll be beating up beautiful women every week."

Susan raised her glass toward me and touched the rim of it against the top of my beer bottle.

She said, "Be my pleasure, big guy."

CHAPTER FIFTY-SIX

The university tenure committee held Robinson Nevins' reconsideration meeting at the university on the third straight day of rain in late August in a room next to the president's office. It was my first tenure meeting. The English department tenure committee, which had originally denied Robinson tenure, had voted not to reconsider, but the university committee, which had the right to overrule the department committee, agreed to a second hearing. This already seemed like several committees more than I wanted anything to do with, but Robinson needed some testimony. Robinson, and Hawk, and I all agreed that it was best not to turn Hawk loose among the academics.

The meeting was chaired by a professor from the Law School named Tillman. I sat against the wall behind Tommy Harmon, who sat at the conference table as Robinson's faculty advocate. Bass Maitland and Lillian Temple were there representing the English department tenure committee. Maitland was speaking in his large rich voice.

"So whatever ex post facto changes may have occurred in the matter of Robinson Nevins' tenure, the department feels that a decision arrived at in good faith should stand. To do otherwise would be to set a precedent that most of us would regret in the years to come."

"Even though the basis for the denial of tenure turned out to be not only unfounded but part of a criminal conspiracy?" Harmon said.

"I believe it is an alleged criminal conspiracy," Maitland said, "until a court of law reaches a judgment."

He leaned back in his chair contentedly. Lillian patted his thigh. Professor Tillman looked a little tired.

He said, "Thank you for the reminder in law, Bass. Tommy, do you have a witness for us?"

Tommy Harmon said he did and introduced me.

"This is not a court of law, and you are not under oath, Mr. Spenser," Tillman said. "Still the business of this committee, which today is particularly serious business, cannot proceed properly if you do not tell the truth."

He was a spare man with a gray crew cut and half glasses. His light tan summer suit looked a little small for him, but you could see that he was not a rube.

"The recommendations of this committee, when they are made, are just that, recommendations," he said. "They are not binding on the university."

Tillman glanced over his half glasses at Bass Maitland. He didn't change his expression, but I got the sense that he and I would agree on Bass.

"But they are not to be cavalierly disregarded either," Tillman said. "There is considerable at stake here."

"I'll try not to lie," I said.

Tillman smiled very slightly.

"Thank you," he said. "We have all, I'm sure, read the papers, but I would like to hear from you what you know, as succinctly as you can. And since I am the chair of this committee, I guess I can. You may remain seated there unless you wish otherwise."

The various professors gathered around the long conference table shifted in their seats a little. Several of them seemed interested. Lillian Temple and Bass Maitland looked resigned to suffering fools as gladly as they could.

"There are police reports," I said. "Both from the Massachusetts State Police who did some of the initial questioning, when Amir Abdullah and Milo Quant were arrested, and from the Boston Police Homicide Unit in whose jurisdiction the murder of Prentice Lamont took place and to whom the state cops turned them over. I assume you all have copies."

Everyone did.

"Okay, here's what I know."

"Excuse me," Bass Maitland said, "I think we'd all be more comfortable if you were a bit more precise in your choice of words. This is what you surmise."

I looked at Bass Maitland for a minute without saying anything. Then I looked back around the table.

"Okay," I said, "here's what I know."

Maitland started to say something and Tillman gestured him to be quiet.

"Prentice Lamont ran a newspaper called *OUTrageous* which, as the name might imply, was in the business of outing closeted gay people. He was also having a sexual affair with Amir Abdullah. Prentice started out high-mindedly, hoping to improve the lot of gay Americans by forcing prominent people who were gay to publicly proclaim themselves. But in a while—Amir has admitted that it was his suggestion—this became a vehicle for blackmail, and made both Amir and Prentice a considerable profit. Amir, however, ever the romantic, lost interest in Prentice and took up with Milo Quant, the head of an anti-gay, anti-black, anti a whole bunch of stuff group called Last Stand Systems, Inc. Prentice, the jilted lover, threatened to out them both if Amir didn't return to his arms. This would work very badly for the man whose official position was white and heterosexual. Amir was frightened about what Milo might do, so without telling Milo, he asked a couple of Milo's security people to shut Prentice up. He swears he thought they'd rough Prentice up and frighten him into silence. The security guys say Amir told them to kill Prentice. Which they did, leaving a kind of all-purpose suicide note."

A thin wiry woman with short very curly hair raised her hand at the far end of the conference table. I nodded at her.

"Did the Last Stand whatchamacallit know about their boss and Amir?"

"No. Just the personal bodyguard. They would smuggle Amir up to a motel near the Maine headquarters, usually, but sometimes to other places, where he would rendezvous with Milo."

"Classic fascist ambivalence," the speaker was a small man with longish tan hair and horn-rimmed glasses, "to lust in private after everything they despise in public."

"You bet," I said. "So Amir decided that since he had a corpse handy, blame Robinson Nevins for it, and get a twofer."

"Excuse me?" Bass Maitland said.

"Two for one," Tillman said brusquely. "Go ahead, Mr. Spenser."

"Well, why on earth would he do that?" Maitland said.

"Amir is pretty pathological," I said. "He couldn't stand any competition, let alone competition from a black scholar as accomplished and as fundamentally decent as Robinson Nevins."

"Nevins never had an affair with Prentice Lamont?" the wiry woman said.

"No. Robinson isn't even gay," I said.

I looked at Lillian Temple. Her face showed nothing.

"Well, for God's sake, why didn't he say so?" Maitland said.

"Because he felt that since the charges were specious regardless of his sexuality, proclaiming his heterosexuality was both undignified and perhaps in some way hostile to the interests of his many gay friends."

"Bass wouldn't understand that," Harmon said.

"Tommy, please," Tillman said.

"I resent that," Maitland said.

"Bass," Tillman said.

"To prove his heterosexuality would have required women to testify that they'd been intimate with him," I said. "Several of them were not free to be. He declined to put them on the spot."

Again I was looking at Lillian Temple. Her appearance remained rigidly unchanged.

"My God," said the little guy with the big glasses, "he sounds like one of nature's noblemen. And we're denying him tenure?"

"Do you know who any of these women are?" the wiry woman asked.

"Yes."

"May we know?"

I shook my head. Lillian Temple's expression remained unchanged. She was so still that she was barely there.

"How do we know that this man is telling the truth?" Maitland said.

"Bass," I said, "I don't wish to appear uncouth, so I'll let it slide that you're kind of calling me a liar. But if you do it outside of these august proceedings, I will knock you on your Harris tweed tookus.''

Tommy Harmon chuckled. Maitland flushed.

''Mr. Spenser,'' Tillman's voice was like the thin edge of a piece of ice. ''Whether or not these proceedings are august, they are serious. Bass, everything Mr. Spenser has said is corroborated in the police reports, generally in Abdullah's own words.''

''I haven't had a chance to read the reports,'' Maitland said sullenly.

''They were distributed three days ago. We all had the chance,'' Tillman said. ''I took advantage of it, you didn't. Do you have anything else to tell us, Mr. Spenser?''

''I have a couple of guesses. One, I think Amir was beginning to tire of Milo. Amir's taste usually ran younger. Or maybe Milo was tiring of Amir. Whatever, Amir proposed the blackmail scheme to Walt and Willie, the two young men who inherited *OUTrageous*. He told them he didn't want a cut. Presumably he didn't need money as long as he was with Milo. But if he was tiring of Milo, or vice versa, or was simply insecure in the covertness of the relationship, and was going to be on his own again, then he'd need to supplement his teaching salary with blackmail money as he had before, and he wanted the system in place. He also took up with one of the young men.''

''Foresighted,'' Tillman said.

The committee asked me maybe a dozen questions. Tommy Harmon spoke about the injustice that they were trying to avert. Bass Maitland made a formal statement about the danger of taking these decisions from the hands of the department. Lillian Temple concurred.

''Are we ready for a vote?'' Tillman said.

They were.

''Very well,'' Tillman said. ''Mr. Spenser, will you step outside, please. Professors Temple, Harmon, Maitland will join him please.''

All the time we stood outside in the corridor nobody said anything. I looked at Lillian Temple. She stood as close as dignity permitted to Bass Maitland and looked at something else. Anything else. I was sort of hoping Bass would call me a liar again. He didn't. Maybe I could put an eraser on my shoulder and dare him to knock it off. I thought about explaining that to Susan afterward, and decided not to dare him.

In about twenty minutes the committee came out in ones and twos and dispersed without saying anything to us. Tillman came out last.

"The committee has voted to recommend to the dean that Robinson Nevins be granted tenure," he said.

Tommy Harmon broke into a wide grin and shook my hand.

"You'll inform Robinson?" I said.

"Right now," he said and walked away.

Bass Maitland and Lillian Temple were still there. He began to walk away. She lingered for a moment behind him.

"Well," she said. "It looks like you've won."

"Yes," I said. "It looks like I have."

"Congratulations."

"Thanks," I said.

"I . . ." She paused for a long time. I waited. Finally she shook her head and turned and started after Maitland.

"Sleep warm," I said.

CHAPTER FIFTY-SEVEN

Apparently it was going to rain forever. But today, so it shouldn't be boring, there was thunder and lightning as well. I was standing at my window watching the rainwater overwhelm the storm drains and back up over the sidewalk on Berkeley Street. A long streak of lightning razzmatazzed across the sky, followed hard upon by thunder. It was early, people were on their way to work. Below me a scatter of colorful umbrella tops was bright against the gleaming wet pavement. Flowers on a dark wet field.

Behind me someone knocked on my office door. I turned away from the storm and looked at the door.

"Come in," I said.

A fat guy with his hat on backward came in.

"You Spenser?" he said.

"Yes."

"Got a couch here."

"A couch?"

"Yeah, where you want it."

"I didn't buy a couch," I said.

"Well, somebody did, says here your name, this address."

"Does it say who bought it?"

"Nope. Got a phone number though."

He read it to me. It was Susan's.

"Put it next to the door," I said.

He went back out and in a minute he came in with one end of a couch wrapped in plastic. At the other end was a tall thin black man who was probably Haitian. They put the couch down, the Haitian man took the plastric wrap off it. The fat guy with the hat got my signature on the slip and they left. I closed the door and looked at the couch. It was very manly looking, brass studs, dark green leather, and long. I tried stretching out on it. Nap-able. I got up and went back and looked at the weather some more. More lightning jittered past. Behind me the door opened. It was Susan wearing a scarlet silk raincoat and a big hat. She had a large bag of something with her. As soon as she got inside she turned and studied the couch.

"Cute, cute, cute, cute, cute," she said.

"Five cutes," I said. "You look like the rain goddess."

"I know," she said. "Do we love our new couch?"

"Cute, cute, cute, cute, cute," I said.

"You've got the phrasing all wrong," she said. "You pause after the second cute, then rattle off the last three rapidly."

"I'll work on it," I said. "What's in the bag?"

"Eats," she said. "In case you've not had breakfast."

"I can always use another breakfast," I said.

"Egg salad sandwiches," Susan said, as she took things out of the bag, and put them on my desk. "On light rye, coffee, and some adorable little Key lime cookies."

"Excellent choices," I said. "Why do I have a new couch in my office?"

"You need one," Susan said.

She put napkins out and unwrapped one of the sandwiches. It was cut in quarters.

"Be nice for Pearl," I said, "next bring your dog to work day."

"Yes, she hates sleeping on the floor."

"Me too," I said. "How come you're not working?"

"I canceled my appointments today, I thought we needed to celebrate."

"Have I missed an anniversary date?" I said.

"No. I just think you've done a hell of a job in some very messy cases that your friends got you into."

The room brightened for a moment as thunder chased lightning past the window. I had a bite of sandwich and a sip of coffee.

"You being one of the friends?" I said.

"And Hawk being the other."

"What are friends for?"

"And Hawk's friend got tenure?" Susan said.

"Yes."

"And Amir whatsisname is going to jail?"

"Pretty sure. Couple of state cops found him hiding naked, trying to get out of the rain, in a culvert under 495. Soon as they got him into the car he started blaming Milo for all his troubles, and along the way confessed to everything. Which works out great because Milo is blaming everything on Amir."

"What about Milo?" Susan said.

"He appears eager to testify against Amir, and the two security guys who tossed Prentice out the window."

"Will he go to jail?"

"I believe him that he didn't know about the Lamont murder," I said. "And since it's not illegal to be a racist gay homophobe, I assume that if the DA believes him, he'll walk when he gets through testifying. His future as a charismatic leader seems grim, though."

We ate a little more sandwich and watched a little more lightning and listened to a little more thunder.

"I know the meteorological explanations," I said to Susan, "and I believe them. But it's hard not to think of the gods during a thunderstorm."

"I know," she said. "And Robinson wasn't even gay."

"Nope."

"But he wouldn't say so."

"Nope."

"That's either great integrity or great foolishness."

"Integrity is often foolish," I said.

She smiled at me and I was thrilled.

"Of course it is," she said. "I understand from sources that KC Roth has gone back to her therapist in Providence."

"Just needed a little professional intervention," I said.

"Didn't you tell me that she asked if you'd ever had sex in the office?"

"Yes."

"And you said you didn't want to do so on the floor, and were waiting for a couch."

"Why yes," I said.

Susan smiled again. Not the smile of approval, which thrilled me, but the smile of promise which could easily launch a thousand ships.

"I believe I see a pattern emerging," I said.

"You're a trained observer," Susan said. "Do you mind making love after you've eaten?"

"After, before, during, instead of—whatever the schedule calls for."

Susan got up and went to my door and locked it. Then she took off her raincoat and hung it on the coatrack. She took her hat off and put it on top of my file cabinet. She slipped her dress over her head, and hung it on a hanger on the rack, taking time to smooth out any wrinkles. She fluffed her hair carefully. Then she turned and smiled at me and finished undressing. She picked up the big hat and put it on.

"Shall we try the couch?" she said.

"With the hat on?" I said.

"Special effects," Susan said.

"Works for me," I said.

The hat was on the floor shortly after we began. The storm made the room sort of dim, except when the lightning made it brilliant. The rain was thick on the window. By the time we finished we were on the floor beside the hat.

"So much for the new couch," I said.

Susan pressed her face into my neck as if her nose were cold.

"So much for KC Roth," she said.

And we lay there with our arms around each other and laughed while the thunder and lightning frolicked with the rain outside.